THE ADVENTURES OF RADISSON 3

THE INCREDIBLE ESCAPE

Martin Fournier

THE ADVENTURES OF RADISSON 3

THE INCREDIBLE ESCAPE

Translated by Peter McCambridge

Baraka Books
Montréal

Originally published as *Les aventures de Radisson – 2 | Sauver les français*

© 2013 Les Éditions du Septentrion, Sillery, Québec (3ᵉ partie)

Translation copyright © Baraka Books

ISBN 978-1-77186-025-3 pbk; 978-1-77186-061-1 epub; 978-1-77186-062-8 pdf; 978-1-77186-063-5 mobi/pocket

Cover by Folio infographie
Cover Illustration by Vincent Partel
Book design by Folio infographie

Legal Deposit, 4th quarter 2015
Bibliothèque et Archives nationales du Québec
Library and Archives Canada

Published by Baraka Books of Montreal.
6977, rue Lacroix
Montréal, Québec H4E 2V4
Telephone: 514 808-8504
info@barakabooks.com
www.barakabooks.com

Printed and bound in Quebec

We acknowledge the support from the Société de développement des entreprises culturelles (SODEC) and the Government of Quebec tax credit for book publishing administered by SODEC.

Société
de développement
des entreprises
culturelles
Québec

We acknowledge the support of the Canada Council for the Arts, which last year invested $153 million to bring the arts to Canadians throughout the country and the support of its National Translation Program for Book Publishing, in initiative of the Roadmap for Canada's Official Languages 2013-2018: Education, Immigration, Communities, for our translation activities.

Financé par le gouvernement du Canada
Funded by the Government of Canada | Canada

Trade Distribution & Returns
Canada and the United States
Independent Publishers Group
1-800-888-4741 (IPG1);
orders@ipgbook.com

CONTENTS

PREVIOUSLY IN *THE ADVENTURES OF RADISSON...*

IN THE SPRING OF 1651, Pierre-Esprit Radisson, a fifteen-year-old from Paris, lands in Trois-Rivières. Within weeks, he is captured by the Iroquois and later adopted as a brother, forging a new life for himself before eventually making his escape.

In Volume 2 of these adventures, Radisson returns to Europe. He signs up with the Jesuits, eager to return to the New World. But doubt begins to set in just as the French prepare to cement their new mission in the heart of Iroquois territory—until recently home to New France's mortal enemy. Can the Iroquois be trusted? Or are their advances nothing more than an elaborate trap?

And now, in Volume 3... well, read on to find out what happens next...

CHAPTER 1

A RUDE AWAKENING

"THEY'RE COMING!" Radisson cried. He was watching around a hundred barechested Iroquois beach their canoes opposite Montréal. They were wearing neither headdress nor war colours. Father Ragueneau ran to meet him.

"My God! Why so many of them?" he wondered out loud, waving his arms to attract their attention.

The Hurons at the camp, a dozen men and some eighty women and children, looked on anxiously.

"Over here!" Father Ragueneau cried. "I'm the one you're meeting!"

Minutes later, a handful of ill-tempered Iroquois were talking with them. They had just crossed the Lachine rapids in their canoes and one had capsized. Five Iroquois had drowned.

Ragueneau tried to find out why they were so late to the meeting but got no answer. Radisson saw no sign of Andoura or any of the other chiefs who had come to negotiate in Trois-Rivières the previous winter. Strange. One of the Iroquois handed Ragueneau a letter from Father Le Moyne that confirmed the French fort was almost completed. The expedition could begin as planned.

But the Iroquois had other ideas. They held a meeting among themselves, demanding that all outsiders keep their distance. Ragueneau started to protest, unhappy at not knowing what they might be plotting, but since some of their men had been killed, he agreed with their request, to avoid offending them.

The meeting went on for a while. Once it was over, they said nothing about what had been discussed.

When talks on organizing the voyage began the following day, the Montrealers kept a watchful eye on the proceedings from a distance, fascinated by the huge gathering of Iroquois, as their spokesman informed Father Ragueneau of the decision made the previous day. He explained that they had put back their departure for a long time. They had travelled very quickly, without stopping to hunt or fish, eating only corn flour to make up for lost time. That's why they had gone through the Lachine rapids instead of portaging their way around them. They were therefore blaming the Frenchmen and the Hurons for the deaths of five of their own and were expecting compensation, which was to be negotiated before they left. Radisson, who was interpreting, passed on the request to Ragueneau, who had already gotten the gist. He replied curtly, in French:

"They have a nerve! Tell him we are prepared to discuss the matter if they agree to transport some of our bags. Our canoes will be fairly weighed down. We need to find a solution."

The Jesuit preferred to hide the fact that his grasp on the Iroquois language was improving, deeming the secret to be to his advantage.

"Be very clear," he added. "We can in no way be held responsible for their blunder, nor for their imprudence, and especially not for their tardiness! They're going too far! We will discuss the matter only to calm them down. And ask them again why they waited so long!"

"I already have, Father. They won't say."

Negotiations were also stuck on how the Hurons were to travel by canoe. The Iroquois wanted to divide the Hurons among them, while Ragueneau demanded the Hurons all travel together in their own canoes, along with the eleven Frenchmen.

On a number of occasions over the course of three long days the exchanges dragged on. Radisson toned down the harsh words used by Ragueneau and his superior Jean de Quen, and he did the same when translating the speech of some of the equally aggressive Iroquois chiefs. There appeared to be two clans. A few chiefs were clearly reluctant to bring the French back with them. Others were making an obvious effort to be pleasant and welcoming to the French. Radisson had trouble making sense of it all.

"Have you noticed they don't all agree?" Radisson asked the Jesuit when they took stock of the situation together.

"It's as though some of them are dragging their feet, while others are trying to win our trust. Can you think why?"

"I can't, Father. It beats me."

"We'll have to keep a close eye on the chiefs who don't like us and do our utmost to keep the others happy."

They came to an agreement on the fourth day. The Frenchmen and the Hurons—who had now joined the negotiations— agreed to give the Iroquois gifts to compensate for the deaths of the five since the accident had happened while coming to fetch them. In return, the Iroquois agreed to transport some of the excess baggage and to allow the Hurons and the French to travel together.

The following day, the last Sunday of July, a great commotion preceded the departure of the two hundred or so people from the shoreline. At the last minute, a dozen carts had to be found to carry the heavier goods above the Lachine rapids, while the French, the Hurons, and the Iroquois trailed their twenty-nine half-filled canoes from the shore. The next day, the flotilla finally set off from the western tip of the island of Montréal.

Like a bear leaving its den in the spring, Radisson's senses came back to life on the trip. At last the real adventure was underway, a big, exciting adventure into unknown territory he couldn't wait to discover.

He sat up at the front of his canoe. Two strapping men with plenty of pluck had recently arrived from France and sat in the middle, while Atahonra, a vastly experienced Huron chief, steered the canoe from the rear. They drove hard to follow the rhythm imposed by the Iroquois who, with seven or eight of them to a canoe, were carrying fewer bags. They had easily taken their place at the head of the expedition. All the canoes behind them were laden with goods and had fewer paddlers, some of them women. It was shaping up to be an arduous journey.

Father Ragueneau had been clear: he wanted Radisson to stick close to the Iroquois to see how they were behaving, and to gauge their mood. In so doing, he hoped to be able to avoid the danger he could sense, rightly or wrongly, beneath the surface.

Even the two Jesuit priests were paddling to keep up the rhythm. They kept to the middle of the canoes, where the going was easier. Robert Racine, one of the old brigade, had lost none of his stamina and steered the canoe Ragueneau was sitting in.

It took them close to two days to cross Lac Saint-Louis and continue upriver where the first big portage waited. Radisson had realized that too many bags would endanger his canoe in choppy water. Once they were all on dry land, he was therefore disconcerted to hear the Iroquois declare they would be carrying their share of the bags no further. Ragueneau was outraged at the turnaround. He demanded they respect the conditions set at the start, but the Iroquois replied it was impossible to continue the journey in such conditions without great risk. The Jesuit ordered the French to block off the portage trail to the Iroquois. They were at an impasse. It was time to renegotiate.

This time, Ragueneau took part in the discussions directly, gabbling a word or two in Iroquois, still trying to mask his real ease with the language. Radisson translated the rest of his speech. The Iroquois' position was clear: the situation was too dangerous; other accidents were inevitable and they intended to avoid them. Ragueneau stressed just how much the French needed all the goods—some of which would later be traded to the Iroquois—but in their eyes nothing justified risking human lives for the sake of the merchandise.

Without saying so openly, Radisson agreed with them. Many articles had been added during the long wait in Montréal, past the limits of common sense. Radisson himself had secretly bought some goods. The Huron chief Atahonra supported the Iroquois: it was not wise to continue in such heavily laden canoes.

Night fell. The French, the Hurons, and the Iroquois lit their fires a short distance from each other. But each stuck to his own group. Only the mosquitoes and the difficult questions hanging over them perturbed the magnificent summer evening.

"It's very serious indeed!" Ragueneau complained, having taken Radisson and Father Jean de Quen aside.

"You're right, Paul," de Quen confirmed. "These goods cost us a fortune. Leaving them here is quite out of the question.

Anyone could walk off with them and then we'd be facing a huge loss. I'll bring them back to Montréal myself, if that's what it takes!"

"I'm growing more and more suspicious of these headstrong Iroquois," Ragueneau added. "They're doing everything they can to be a thorn in our side. I wonder if we're going to be able to get along with them after all."

Radisson could see the resignation on the faces of his superiors, who fell silent for a long time. Only the distant murmurs of the *voyageurs* and the crackling of the fire could be heard. He decided the time had come to chip in with his own opinion.

"We are carrying too much, Father. Atahonra and the Iroquois are right. What will we gain by losing part of the load and sacrificing lives along the way?"

Ragueneau did not reply.

"I fear I must return to Montréal," de Quen sighed. "You are better prepared than I to serve in Iroquois lands. Go on ahead, Paul. I don't see any other way out of this mess. I'll bring back some of the goods along with two or three Frenchmen. Keep the most experienced men. Unless you have another solution?"

Ragueneau would have preferred not to go along with such a disappointing proposal. But he could not see any other way out either. Montréal was still close and four men would quite easily be able to navigate their way to Lachine with two large canoes filled to the limit. If they chose less important goods and inexperienced men, it would barely have an impact on the expedition.

"Very well," Ragueneau concluded. "Let's go back and negotiate this compromise with the Iroquois. But in return we'll ask them to keep their side of the bargain and carry some of the load. Be as convincing as you can, Radisson. We have no more ground to give."

Early the next day, Radisson supervised as the bags were sorted, making sure to keep the trading goods with him. Non-essentials were loaded onto two big canoes belonging to the French. Those continuing on the voyage bade farewell to Father de Quen and his crew of three. Spirits were low once they left. But it wasn't the time to let heads go down. They pulled themselves together and portaged all the material beyond the rapids, where another disappointment lay in store.

The Iroquois agreed to carry the goods provided the French travelled with them. Ragueneau had to face facts: he had lost control. Tension rose another notch when five of the seven remaining Frenchmen found themselves in five separate canoes. Only Father Ragueneau was allowed to stay with Robert Racine, along with a Huron man and two Huron women.

At least the expedition was moving forward.

For the first time in years, Radisson found himself alone with a group of five Iroquois. It didn't take him long to settle in. The going was easy. Radisson had been put in the middle of the canoe and his sole responsibility was to paddle regularly, without overly exerting himself. He conserved his energy and concentrated on the task Ragueneau had set him: keeping an eye on the Iroquois. With their bulging muscles and proud demeanour, his well-built companions paddled as one and spoke little. From time to time, one of them pointed out an obstacle to avoid, a fish jumping out of the water, or an animal that appeared on the shore.

His companions were aware that Radisson had mastered the Iroquois language, but they did not know where he had learned it. They did not suspect he had been adopted by a family from the Bear clan and had spent two years in a Mohawk village. They had no inkling that he had fought at their side. Radisson was proud of the experience—he could still hear Orinha, his Iroquois name, ringing in his ears—even though he had turned his back on this episode in his life. He felt safe in the knowledge that he could tell them at any moment about his adoptive parents and the war expedition he had taken part in. Since he was a skilled and strong paddler with plenty of stamina, he was treated with respect.

At the camp that night, as on previous days, the French, the Hurons, and the Iroquois split into separate groups. Only Radisson felt comfortable. The situation was very different for the Hurons and the other Frenchmen, who could feel how far the Iroquois were able to impose their laws. Suspicion was in the air more than ever. Father Ragueneau turned to Radisson for advice.

"Do you think we can trust them?"

"Perhaps. They've already had us make a lot of concessions. They seem satisfied now. It's an encouraging sign. We'll see what tomorrow brings."

"I don't like being under their control. Or having to obey their every whim. The least they could do is keep their word. Otherwise why waste all this time negotiating?"

"The next time," Radisson suggested, "go about things the right way. Exchange gifts with them, as you do when concluding an important agreement. That might help."

After a moment's thought, Ragueneau added:

"Did you notice their emissaries didn't give me a gift this winter when they came to Trois-Rivières?"

"Worst of all, none of them came to fetch us."

"Bizarre."

"It's not normal..."

Radisson promised himself to be even more vigilant. Something wasn't right, but he couldn't put his finger on it.

The next day, everything went well. Everyone took their place in the same canoe as the previous day. The Iroquois had no new requests and nothing to complain about. Navigating their way along this part of the river was easy. There were no obstacles and the region they were passing through was beautiful. The day brought with it a certain comfort. Two Iroquois who had forged ahead killed a deer along the way. When night fell, they shared the meat with the French and the Hurons.

"I have never been to this region before," Ragueneau admitted as he enjoyed his share of the meat. "I always took the rivière des Outaouais to get to the Hurons. Here was enemy territory. I would never have dared venture here."

"Our guides say there is a lot of game in the surrounding area. Many are going to spend the day hunting tomorrow. It seems there is very good fishing to be had, too, a little further on."

"There's no need. We've lost enough time as it is. If the land of the Iroquois is as rich as they say, we will have plenty of other opportunities to have a fine time of it. Tell them we are pressed for time."

Radisson got up just as the sun was clearing the horizon. He saw that thirty or so Iroquois had disappeared with their canoes. They had left in silence during the night, or at the crack of dawn, without waking a single Huron or Frenchman. No one had mentioned the day before that so many of them would be leaving to go hunting. As the rest of the camp came to life, Radisson walked among the Iroquois, asking one for an extra pot, another for a piece of string or roots, which gave him a chance to spy on them.

"Where did your brothers go?"

The answers varied. Some said to hunt, others to fish, still others explained that a group had gone on ahead to prepare that evening's camp. The vague and varied information he obtained, without raising undue suspicion, got Radisson thinking. He even caught a few snatches of conversation that suggested another theory.

"Have you noticed there are around thirty Iroquois missing?" he asked Ragueneau when he came back.

"Of course I have! Atahonra is worried. He came to talk to me about it."

"They don't all say the same thing when I ask where they've gotten to. I'm sure they're hiding something from us, Father. I heard a few things and I fear some of them have gone off to fight the Algonquins, or other allies of ours who are not included in the peace."

"Things are going from bad to worse."

"We need to be more careful than ever, Father. Keep your eyes open. Something strange is going on."

Several Iroquois exchanged knowing glances and whispered among themselves when Radisson joined them in the canoe. Once they were out on the river, they fell silent. They seemed more tense than the day before. Late that morning, Radisson pretended he couldn't find something in his bags and asked his companions to wait for Father Ragueneau's canoe to see if it was in his. The truth was he wanted to make sure the canoes did not get too far apart.

An hour later, a canoe that had been lagging behind, abruptly turned around. It was carrying five women and led by a Huron warrior. Its passengers threw all they had been carrying overboard and paddled off as fast as they could. By the time the Iroquois realized what was happening, it was too late to catch them. But the Iroquois seemed troubled by the incident and stayed where they were for a long while.

The four Iroquois by his side appeared crestfallen and Radisson was convinced they would have liked to give chase, but neither he nor the Huron with them—who appeared completely taken aback—would have agreed.

The flotilla set off again, at last.

The Huron desertion seemed to be forgotten. That afternoon, the Iroquois sitting beside Radisson in the canoe pointed out a deer drinking on the shore.

"I'm going hunting when we reach camp," he said, briefly clutching his rifle. "We shall eat well tonight."

Further on, Radisson could see huge fish in the crystal-clear water. They would be easy to spear. He pointed them out.

"We could fish, too."

"Good idea!" the Iroquois agreed. "We'll have a real feast!"

The sun dropped in the sky. A thin layer of clouds turned pink and orange above the horizon. The calm surface of the water glistened beneath the sacred star's reflection. A slight breeze caressed the *voyageurs'* backs. Two canoes pulled up onto a fine sandy beach and a handful of Iroquois jumped out. After a time, three shots rang out. Radisson looked on as the hunters returned, trailing a young deer behind them, to the delight of those waiting for them on the shore. The area in which they were to spend the night was exceptionally beautiful and lush.

The canoes at the front were banked on the beach of a large island in the middle of the river. The Iroquois who jumped out motioned for the others to join them, but the leader of Radisson's canoe steered them to the opposite shore. Once they were beached in the tall grass, the Iroquois sitting up front jumped out with his musket. He hadn't taken two steps when he whirled around and fired from point-blank range at the Huron sitting in front of Radisson. The warrior fell to the ground, gasping. Another Iroquois stood over him and cracked open his skull with a tomahawk. Blood flooded across the bottom of the canoe and onto the feet of Radisson, who was so stunned he had not moved.

The Iroquois who had fired the shot told him "You have nothing to fear" before running across to the other side of the island, screaming all the way. His three companions bounded out of the canoe, without giving the Frenchman another thought. They also ran off, crying, too, as though possessed. Sweat ran down Radisson's back. He still had not moved. Stunned at the sight of the Huron who lay dying at his feet, he brought a trembling hand to his knife and unsheathed it. Some of his composure returned when he set foot on dry land again, his legs weak as rags.

He followed the Iroquois' trail, his knife held out in front, a laughable defence against their muskets. His favourite weapon nonetheless reassured him. In the distance, he could hear women whimpering and children crying. When he reached the island's highest point, he hid in the undergrowth. From there, he could see the Huron women huddled together like a flock of sheep against a pack of wolves set to devour them. They cried before dozens of armed, menacing Iroquois, who had them surrounded. Young children took shelter among them. Between the defenceless women and the Iroquois, ten Huron men were trying to stand up to their attackers. They were armed only with tomahawks and knives. None of them had as much as a bow with which to oppose the Iroquois' muskets. Father Ragueneau was also trying to protect the women, holding out his arms in a cross in front of them and glowering at the assailants.

Radisson had no idea how things had gotten to this point. Everything had happened so quickly. The Huron's murder had left him fearing the worst. Alone with his knife, he did not know how he could possibly prevent a massacre.

A chief slipped in between the Hurons and the group of forty or so Iroquois. He walked up to one of his own and began to reason with him. Carefully, he took away the tomahawk he had been brandishing over his head and flung it to the ground. He went on talking to his warriors, his back turned to Radisson, who could only hear the sound of his voice, without being able to make out what was said. The women were now almost silent. When he at last turned back around, Radisson could hear the chief proposing to the Hurons that they forget the incident and put up their shelters for the night, as though nothing had happened. But nobody budged. Not the Hurons, not the Iroquois, not Ragueneau. His speech didn't seem to have had any effect. The tension had reached breaking point.

Further along the beach, Radisson discovered the five other Frenchmen taking cover behind their canoes. In fact, all he could see was their muskets, pointed at the Iroquois. He would have liked to run and join them to get a firearm of his own, but he feared he might attract the attention of an overly nervous Iroquois. So, in order not to frighten anyone, he picked himself up again slowly, emerged carefully from the undergrowth and, calmly at first then with increasing urgency, walked over to his French companions. Ragueneau did not even notice him. The Iroquois paid him no heed. As soon as he was in line with the canoes, Dufresne grabbed him by the arm and hauled him to the ground beside him.

"Get down, you idiot!"

Racine noticed his blood-covered feet.

"What happened to you?"

"I'm fine," Radisson replied, still stunned. "It's the blood of the Huron who was with me. They killed him, shot him close up."

"The snakes!" Dufresne exclaimed.

Suddenly the thirty Iroquois who had disappeared that morning came running out of the bushes, crying and covered in war paint. They rushed at the Huron warriors. Dufresne got off a shot in their direction. Radisson and the four other Frenchmen stayed where they were, dumfounded. The fight was as ferocious as it was unfair. In seconds, the ten Hurons had been torn to shreds by a hundred tomahawk and knife wounds. Piercing shrieks from the women could be heard over the clamour of combat.

Then a heavy silence fell over the island.

Ten bodies lay on the ground, hacked to pieces. A single Iroquois had perished, his body lying among the Hurons. No one moved for a moment that seemed to last an eternity, then a few Iroquois began dragging the Huron bodies to the river. With utter disregard, they cast them adrift at once, like rotten carcasses. The current carried them far into the distance. Satisfied, the Iroquois recovered their victim and carried him to the centre of the island, where they calmly prepared their camp.

The Huron women formed a compact, silent huddle. They kept their eyes glued to the ground, clutching their distraught children. Looking on helplessly, an incredulous Father Ragueneau had not moved. Radisson was concerned at his master's attitude. Did he still want to protect the Huron women? Was he prepared to die for them? The Jesuit watched bitterly as the Iroquois set up their camp. No one paid them any attention, not even the chief who had seemed to want to avoid the massacre—or perhaps help bring it about through trickery. Radisson could see not the slightest sign of remorse among them. At the same time, all danger seemed to have passed.

He thought back to Pierre Godefroy's warning: "The Iroquois want only to weaken us..." He had been right. They had eliminated only the Huron warriors who had posed a threat to them. Even though he had had a bad feeling since the outset, never would Radisson have suspected scores to be settled in such radical fashion, right under the nose of Father Ragueneau, who had reached an agreement with them over adopting the Hurons. That was the Iroquois way he knew—surprise and strength, cunning and swiftness—that had brought the small group victories over the Erie.

Radisson had learned a lesson. Being wary of the Iroquois was not enough. They had to be beaten at their own game, with speed and cunning. Otherwise they had the upper hand.

His head was abuzz with ideas as his companions prepared to fight the Iroquois "dogs," as Dufresne had put it. He did not share their fear of falling victim to the Iroquois' deadly violence: Radisson would already be dead, if they had wanted to kill him. No Frenchmen had been threatened during the attack either. The French and the Iroquois were still at peace.

"They'll soon see what they're up against," Dufresne hissed through gritted teeth.

"Take a musket," Racine ordered. "They're going to attack us."

Radisson rummaged around in the bags to find the muskets they had been going to trade with the Iroquois. He took one, loaded it, and set it against the canoe. He did the same with another. His companions followed suit. In no time at all, they had sixteen muskets ready to fire. If the Iroquois attacked, Racine would reload them as needed. Then they piled up packages around them to protect themselves from all sides.

Once ready, Radisson looked on at a scene that seemed completely unreal to him. The Iroquois had lit fires and were preparing their meals as if nothing had happened. A small group fed the funeral pyre where they would burn their dead warrior. A shaman cloaked in wolf skin performed a cleansing ceremony as a final tribute to the warrior and to help him return to the land of his ancestors.

Between the Iroquois and the Frenchmen taking cover behind the canoes, Father Ragueneau had at last sat down beside the Huron women, who were whispering among themselves. Radisson looked at him closely. He wondered if he should wait until the Jesuit motioned to him or if he should make the first move and walk over to him. He didn't know how to ease his master's suffering and distress. He chose to wait.

Night fell. Radisson's companions gathered wood to light a fire, but they preferred to remain in darkness to keep a closer eye on the Iroquois. Radisson prepared a few bark torches so they could move around more easily during the night. He vowed to bring one to Father Ragueneau. He would use the opportunity to try to talk him into joining them. His master couldn't spend the night where he was. Nor could the Hurons, for that matter.

Two Iroquois chiefs came down from their camp to speak with the Jesuit. They invited him to join them, with the Hurons and the other Frenchmen. They had made something to eat, and shelters for everyone. The two chiefs promised that the rest of the trip would pass by without incident. They asked Ragueneau to take part in a meeting they would be holding at any moment. As soon as they went back to their camp, Radisson went over to his master.

"There you are," Ragueneau said. "Where did you go?"

"What did the Iroquois say?"

"They invited us to eat with them. Imagine... after all that's just happened. Do you think we should go?"

Radisson could barely make out his master's face in the ever-darkening half-light. He seemed disheartened.

"They killed the Huron who was in the canoe with me," Radisson replied. "They could have killed me, too. But they didn't. An Iroquois told me I had nothing to fear. I think we can trust them. They were angry with the Huron warriors. Not with us. Not with the women either."

"Perhaps," Ragueneau sighed. "They just told me exactly that."

The two men each took a moment to think things through. The Hurons were still debating among themselves which was the greater risk: going back to the Iroquois or staying off to one side with no means of support.

A half-moon stood out in a now almost black sky.

"I brought you a torch, Father. You'll need it."

"Thank you," the Jesuit replied, taking the torch without thinking.

An elderly Huron woman came up to the priest and stared at him. Ragueneau took a while to notice her.

"Yes, Tsahoni?"

"We have decided to go back to the Iroquois as long as you come with us."

Ragueneau lowered his head in thought.

"Very well, let us go," he replied after a moment.

He turned to Radisson.

"Are you coming with us? The two chiefs asked me to take part in a meeting. I believe I will need you to translate what they say. In my present state, I fear I will not understand a word."

"I will come with you, Father. Please give me a moment. I will try to convince the others to come with us."

"Good idea. We will be stronger if we all stay together."

Dufresne spat on the ground in response to the invitation.

"I'd rather starve to death than walk into their trap! If you want to get yourselves killed, go right ahead!"

Robert Racine was more nuanced, but thought it best to remain holed up where they were. Up against five well-armed men who had barricaded themselves away, the Iroquois would think twice before betraying the men they called their allies.

"We're staying here. We'll protect you," Racine replied.

"As you wish."

Radisson went back alone to Ragueneau and the Hurons. They walked over to the Iroquois camp together.

The Jesuit was not hungry. He went over immediately to sit with the chiefs who had begun their meeting. He interrupted them, asking them to once again provide him with explanations and guarantees. Radisson joined them shortly afterwards, still devouring the piece of roasted venison he had picked up on the way. They said they had killed the Hurons to avenge their warriors who had died in the Lachine rapids and promised that no member of the expedition, Frenchman or Huron, would be mistreated. They also pledged to look after the Huron women, as they were that evening, and to welcome them with open arms onto their lands. Ragueneau was half-satisfied with their response and demanded that each of the seven chiefs personally confirm this commitment as they looked him in the eye. Once they had all repeated the promise, he stood up.

"Wait for me here, Radisson. This time *I'll* try to persuade the others to join us."

Carrying a torch and a hunk of meat, the Jesuit walked over slowly to the five Frenchmen's makeshift stronghold. They recognized him from a good distance away, but remained on their guard because the light from his torch was preventing them from getting a clear look at their enemies.

"You can come over," the Jesuit told them. "It's the Hurons they had a problem with. No women, no Frenchmen will be harmed. Seven chiefs have just given me their word."

"The lowlifes," muttered Dufresne under his breath.

"You trust them, if you want," Racine replied. "We'll be staying put. Now please put out your torch, Father, or go back to them. We can't see them with the light from your torch."

"Father," Ragueneau thought to himself. It sounded so strange. He was a missionary, taking care of the people of Trois-Rivières, a place without a parish let alone a parish priest. It seemed so out of place. But this was no time to make petty distinctions.

"At least come eat something," he told them. "You need to get your strength back."

"Tomorrow, Father. Now put out your torch or go. We're not budging."

The other Frenchmen kept their silence to show they agreed with Racine, who had become the group's leader.

"As you wish," Ragueneau concluded. "I'll leave you this meat. Good night."

"See you later, Father. Thanks all the same."

"O ye of little faith," the Jesuit thought to himself on his way back to the camp.

As he ate a mouthful or two around the fire, Ragueneau did not say a word. He looked serious. Radisson stayed by his side, ready for any eventuality, his musket resting in his lap. None of the Iroquois batted an eyelid. They were all very calm, as though nothing had happened. The Hurons stayed quiet and off to one side. Even their children did not make a sound.

When the Jesuit stopped picking at his food, he asked Radisson to go fetch the three wampums the Hurons had brought with them to give to the Iroquois when they arrived. The time for formalities had passed. He told Radisson where the shell necklaces were, wrapped in a bark-covered package with a turtle drawn on it. As Radisson walked off, torch in hand and his musket slung across his shoulder, the Jesuit went back to the seven chiefs and called another meeting.

Radisson was more prudent than his master and shouted at his companions from a distance:

"Don't shoot! It's me!"

He planted his torch in the sand and rummaged through the scattered bags. He went as fast as he could: his five companions were very much on edge. Racine remembered having seen the package as they had prepared their defences and found it in no time. Radisson headed back right away.

Father Ragueneau began the negotiations in Iroquois himself. Radisson helped him, completing or clarifying his thoughts. The chiefs were impressed to hear the Jesuit speak with such aplomb, his voice still laced with bitterness but powerful. He threw a first wampum at the feet of the seven Iroquois sitting by the fire.

"I am giving you this present so that we might preserve the friendship between the French and the Onondaga. I am prepared to forget what happened today as long as you swear you are still at peace with us. Do you accept my gift?"

The Iroquois glanced at each other and replied "Ho! Ho!" in turn to show they accepted the gift and the meaning Ragueneau had attached to it.

The Jesuit took another necklace from Radisson and again flung it to the ground, near the fire. He continued in a tone that grew firmer still, half his words in French, asking Radisson to translate as required.

"I give you this second gift to require that you take care of all the Huron women and children who are still with us. May you treat them as your own. You will adopt them as soon as you arrive in your country. I want them to be well treated. Do not make slaves of them, as has happened in the past, otherwise you shall feel the wrath of the Great Spirit of the French, who is listening to me as I speak. Do it out of love for us. We are your friends and agreed to hand over the Hurons to you.

You massacred those Hurons without shame, even though I loved them as brothers. If peace is broken between us, it will be your fault. So do you accept this gift? Do you promise to adopt the Hurons and treat them well?"

The chiefs again glanced at each other. They had already made this promise at the previous meeting. But they could see that Ragueneau was having real trouble believing them. One of the chiefs brought up past negotiations.

"Last winter, our emissaries asked you to adopt the Hurons to form one sole people with us. You agreed. Earlier, we promised you none of them would be mistreated. Those we killed had to die to avenge our dead and calm the angry spirits. Now they are at peace. You no longer have anything to worry about. All the women will be looked after. They will become Iroquois as though they had been born to our mothers and fathers. We accept the wampum and renew our promise."

The other chiefs agreed with a heartfelt "Ho! Ho!" The Jesuit took the third necklace and set it more gently at the feet of the chief who had just spoken.

"This third gift is to ask you to lead us quickly back to your lands, now that the going is smooth. Promise me you'll see to it that nothing you carry is lost, stolen, or left behind. Treasure it: these bags are precious for us and for you. Do you accept my third gift?"

The chiefs acquiesced with a unanimous "Ho! Ho!"

"May God be with us," Ragueneau concluded, somewhat relieved.

He turned to Radisson.

"Tell them that from now on I want to see three of them always wearing one of these wampums lest they forget their promises. It will be proof of their sincerity. Tell them I insist."

Radisson translated his words.

"We will wear them to please our French friends," replied the chief acting as spokesperson. "Do not worry. Before long, we will be arriving in our country with all your goods. All will be well."

The meeting was over. One of the chiefs threw a little tobacco on the fire before getting up. Radisson took it to be a good sign. This time everything had followed established procedure. They retired to their shelters for the night.

CHAPTER 2

TO THE BITTER END

THE FOLLOWING DAY, things got off to a slow start. The five Frenchmen who had cut themselves off from the rest of the group categorically refused to team up with the Iroquois. They would go on, but only if they could all be in the same canoe. That was not negotiable. In return, Radisson and Ragueneau agreed to travel in separate canoes with an Iroquois crew. The Jesuit also had to get the Huron women to agree to an Iroquois leading their canoe, with two others helping them paddle, otherwise they would have slowed down the entire expedition. They consented until one of them recognized one of the Iroquois who had killed their husbands. This time, their decision was final. It took several hours of discussions and adjustments to strike a balance and calm the tensions still very much alive after the massacre.

As they divided up the bags again, more than once Radisson made eye contact with his master. He saw great distress in his eyes, an enormous void that the Jesuit was impressively managing to keep under control. Since that morning, Ragueneau had been supervising everything, negotiating with each party, giving orders, making the men leading each canoe aware of their responsibilities. He even found the strength to comfort the most grief-stricken Hurons.

As he watched him, Radisson could see the spark that still burned within the Jesuit. It was incredibly intense, like pure water at the bottom of a deep, dark well. It gave Radisson the energy he needed to assist his master. Ragueneau was helping Radisson's courage return, just as his Iroquois father had done during his torture. True strength came from adversity. This setback wouldn't stop them. Not him, not Ragueneau. They would keep on going, right to the end. Both were cut from the same cloth.

The afternoon was well underway when the expedition got moving. Radisson was again careful to keep his trading goods close. He was now travelling with two Iroquois in the flotilla's smallest canoe. Sorense, the youngest and sturdiest of his new companions, was the same age as Radisson. They bantered back and forth. Sorense was always keen to prove that the Iroquois were the best and could do better than the French. He was more skilful, he boasted, stronger and wiser than Radisson, who was having none of it and was determined to prove him wrong.

Two days later, the Iroquois accompanying them changed canoes to compensate for a man who had fallen ill and could no longer paddle. Radisson and Sorense found themselves alone. Despite the lighter bags, they fell far behind the rest of the expedition. The teasing quickly became reproachful, each accusing the other of paddling like a woman, taking things easy, being clumsy... As they dragged their canoes around a rapid, Radisson voiced real annoyance at Sorense's nonchalance.

"Come on, you lazy good-for-nothing! At this rate, we'll never catch up!"

"I couldn't care less," Sorense replied. "At least I know the way. That's more than you can say, little Frenchman."

"I said, let's go!"

"I'm not going to be bossed around by the likes of you!"

Sorense shoved Radisson back onto the rocks. He leapt straight back up and struck Sorense as hard as he could. The Iroquois replied in kind. A skirmish ensued, during which they let go of the rope to their canoe, which was swept off by the current. The two broke off from their fight to watch the canoe race across the rapids. As he watched his precious trading goods and musket drift off into the distance, Radisson's anger exploded. He launched himself at the Iroquois.

"You savage! It's all your fault!"

The tussle was brief and violent. Then both realized the predicament they were in, far from the rest of the expedition, without food or weapons. They stopped. It was no time to get hurt or waste energy. They peered anxiously at the foot of the rapids to see what had happened to the canoe. Radisson thought he could see it, still afloat in the middle of the river.

"Follow me," he said to Sorense. "Let's go get it."

Sorense would have walked in the other direction to catch up with the group ahead of them. But they had fallen so far behind the thought filled him with little enthusiasm. He too thought he could glimpse the canoe in the middle of the river and so he followed Radisson.

As luck would have it, the canoe hadn't capsized. It was washed up on a sandbank some three hundred feet from shore. Sorense didn't want to risk swimming out so far. He was afraid they might drown. Radisson was prepared to give it a shot, but he had never swum so far. First he estimated the pull of the current so as not to be swept off too far. Then he walked a little upstream, took off his clothes, walked out as far as he could into the river, and began to dog-paddle. The current wasn't especially strong. The sandbank seemed within reach. But he was tiring quickly. Keep going, can't give up now, my life depends on it... He tried to find a foothold but the water was still too deep. He swallowed a mouthful and spluttered. He was struggling against the current as it began to carry him off... He dove forward, grabbed hold of some plants growing in the river, caught his breath, and back on the sandy bottom crawled until he at last reached the beach.

Radisson wasted no time in pulling the canoe further out of the water to stop it from drifting off again. Then, exhausted from all the risk and effort, not to mention the fight, he sat down with an overwhelming feeling of loneliness. He rested for a long while, thinking of Father Ragueneau and the other Frenchmen whose company he so craved. Now and again he glanced over at Sorense. He was gesticulating at him from the shore, waving his arms wildly and whooping with joy, but Radisson had no desire to go back to his conceited companion. The sun set on the horizon in a dazzling sky. Fortunately, they had so far enjoyed good weather for the whole expedition.

One bright spot amidst all the difficulties.

After checking the canoe's condition, Radisson made his way back to Sorense. They slept right there and left at dawn.

It was tough travelling apart from the rest of the expedition, almost always in silence, and with no real rapport with his companion. Radisson again began to question the reasons for making the trip. From the very start, he had been confronted with the one thing he didn't like about the Iroquois: their violent ways. He was eager to be reunited with Father Ragueneau, a man he respected. He still harboured hopes of clearing up his relationship to the eagle and, with a little luck, he would learn where Andoura had gotten his knife. Perhaps he would also be able to trade a little, too. But his heart was no longer in it.

Soon they caught up with four Iroquois who had stayed behind to wait for them: Ononta (the sick man who could no longer paddle), his wife, their son, and Tehagonra, who had travelled with them for two days. Their progress was very slow. Ononta spent two whole days trying to get his strength back in a sweat lodge. No one complained because he seemed to be well respected, but the prolonged wait removed any hopes Radisson had of catching up with the other Frenchmen.

Sorense was back to being his arrogant self. On rare occasions, he and Radisson still enjoyed teasing each other, but more often than not their rivalry led to confrontation. Sorense made sure to disagree with Radisson no matter what he said. And whenever they all ate together at camp in the evenings, Tehagonra was always talking about how superior the Iroquois were. Radisson was sure he had been one of the group who had ambushed and killed the Hurons. One evening, he confronted him about it.

"Why did you kill the Hurons?"

"They got what they deserved," Tehagonra replied proudly as he looked up.

Radisson was feeling less safe as time went on. Only Mahatari, Ononta's wife, was nice to him. He slept badly and was constantly on his guard, which drained all his strength. His desire to be with his French companions, to eat and laugh with them, to tell them all about his misadventures and hear about their own was becoming an obsession. He thought about them all day long and sometimes felt disheartened.

At the end of the eighth day spent with the five Iroquois, they beached their two canoes to set up camp and discovered, in a place used by other *voyageurs* some days earlier, a drawing of six decapitated men on a piece of bark. One of the men had short hair like the Jesuits, which was rare in this country. Radisson concluded that the six other Frenchmen on the expedition had been massacred and began to shake uncontrol-lably. Overcome by the thought that he was going to die, he immediately slid the unloaded musket from across his shoulder down into his hands. The gesture seemed a little pointless. The Iroquois he was up against would have finished him off ten times by the time he managed to fire.

Sorense and Tehagonra burst out laughing. Those weren't Frenchmen in the drawing, they said. They were at peace with them. Radisson had nothing to fear, they told him as they shoved him, laughing. Radisson dropped his musket and took out his eagle-head knife, pointing it at them while shaking like a leaf. The Iroquois countered by aiming their loaded muskets at him. Radisson didn't stand a chance. He could picture himself tied up against the torture post again. The thought paralyzed him.

Tehagonra and Sorense continued to poke fun at him. One ran behind him and called for him to watch out. Radisson turned around. The other gave out a war cry, and Radisson turned back around. He literally didn't know which way to turn. Sorense waited for Radisson to turn his back then charged at him and wrestled the knife from his grip.

"By my father Garagonké!" Radisson cried. "Give me back my knife!"

"Just let me take a quick look," Sorense replied smoothly. "You know that we are brothers. We're supposed to share everything."

"By my mother Katari and my brother Ganaha, give it back! I am Orinha. The Iroquois of the Bear clan adopted me. I am one of your own..."

Ononta suddenly turned toward them, stood up, and cried: "Stop it, both of you!"

The two younger Iroquois stopped fooling around right away. Ononta walked over to them.

"Give me that knife," he told Sorense.

He took a long look at it, then handed it back to Radisson. "Put it away and come eat."

But Radisson didn't dare touch the food Mahatari had prepared, in case they were trying to poison him.

After only a few mouthfuls, Ononta got up from his meal and asked Radisson to take him across to the other shore in the canoe. The invalid borrowed Tehagonra's loaded musket and Tehagonra came with them too. Radisson followed them begrudgingly, recalling the Huron who had been killed right in front of him in the canoe. The same fate surely awaited him. The fear was unbearable. He paddled half-heartedly, ashamed at being such easy prey. As soon as they reached the shore, Ononta moved off, motioning for them to be silent. He disappeared into the woods. After a moment that seemed to go on forever, Radisson gave a start as an explosion rang out. No one had shot at him, thank God. He was still alive. Ononta soon reappeared, carrying a dead eagle. Radisson couldn't believe that a man he had never seen hunt had managed to bring down an eagle so easily.

Back at the camp, Ononta asked Radisson to hand him his knife again. He refused. But the man stared at him so insistently, pointing to the eagle he had just shot, that Radisson couldn't help but give it to him. Ononta looked at the sculpted handle from all angles, then walked off with the dead eagle and the knife. From a distance, Radisson watched him carefully handle the bird, pronouncing words that he couldn't quite make out. He feared he might be draining his favourite weapon of all its powers or casting a bad spell on him. Perhaps he had fallen victim to an evil sorcerer.

Sorense and Tehagonra starting laughing at him again. They pushed and shoved at him, provoked him, made him look ridiculous. Radisson couldn't find the strength to defend himself. He wanted to run off to bring the torture to an end, but it was beyond him. Mahatari came to his rescue.

"Stop it! That's enough. Come here, you."

Radisson followed her to the tent, like a child. She ordered him inside, took the knife out of her husband's hands, and gave it back to Radisson.

"Sleep here. That's not Frenchmen in the drawing. No one's going to kill you."

Radisson lay down on the ground. Mahatari threw a bear-skin over his head. She lay down next to him.

"Now sleep!" she ordered, holding him tight in her arms.

Radisson was still afraid he was going to die, but at least this way he would leave this world in a woman's arms or while he was sleeping. He fell into a deep sleep.

When he awoke, Radisson was surprised to still be alive. He was all alone in the small birch-bark teepee, already warm from the beating sun. He listened to his companions chatting around the fire, just steps away. They were surely ready to leave. He knew they would make fun of him when he went back out, but he was no longer afraid. He took the time to enjoy the smells of bark, balsam, and fur that filled the teepee. He took a deep breath, wondering at the light that leaked through the leather flap covering the door. How wonderful it felt to be alive! He grabbed his eagle-head knife for reassurance. The energy that flooded through him convinced him that Ononta had not neutralized its powers. His companions had been telling the truth: they wished him no harm.

Radisson nonetheless mulled over the strange coincidence. What were the chances of this man shooting an eagle at that very moment, with a single shot? Might Ononta have magical powers? Might he be a shaman?

Aside from a sarcastic comment or two, the day went well. Sorense left him alone as they paddled at a steady pace. At twilight, Ononta again went off by himself, taking the dead eagle with him. Radisson couldn't see what he was doing, but he did hear him chanting, although the words were just as incomprehensible as the previous night. Mahatari again had the Frenchman sleep in the same tent as she and her family. She asked him where he had learned to speak Iroquois. Radisson told her how Katari and Garagonké had adopted him to replace their son Orinha. She listened as he told her about his life in the Bear clan longhouse, the expedition he had gone on to Erie territory, and the honours he had received upon his return, until sleep overcame them.

For the next few days, Radisson travelled with Mahatari and Ononta. Sorense and Tehagonra took the other canoe together.

At last they emerged onto a huge lake and made easy progress to the mouth of a fast-flowing river on the south shore. After three days of hard work travelling upriver, Radisson at last caught sight of the French fort. He was so moved that he could not speak.

"Gannentaha," Mahatari said to him, pointing to the fort. "You have arrived."

Radisson had tears in his eyes as he saw men dressed in *Canadien* style bustle around the fort. After the previous summer's dashed hopes, Pierre Godefroy's doubts, the Huron massacre, and Radisson's own fear that he would be next to lose his life, he had finally reached his goal in Iroquois country.

"There he is!" shouted a man on the shore. "It's Radisson! Here he comes!"

All the Frenchmen working outside the fort hurried to him. Others emerged from inside through the large open gate. They gathered on the shore, shouting with joy as they watched the last missing Frenchman arrive. Radisson was excited by the boisterous welcome. Clambering out of the canoe, he embraced everyone in turn, happy to again be with his own people and speaking his language. Father Ragueneau arrived and held out his arms to him.

"What a relief!" he exclaimed. "I was so worried! Whatever happened to you, for the love of God?"

"Nothing serious, Father. Ononta was ill and slowed us down. I'll tell you all about it later."

Mahatari, Ononta, and their son were waiting in silence in the canoe on the shore. Radisson went back to them to unload the bags. He carried his trading goods himself, giving the other parcels to the men from the fort. Then he thanked Ononta and Mahatari for their help and asked where they lived so that he could visit them.

"In the village of Onondaga, less than a day from here," Mahatari replied. "You'll always be welcome in our home. It's your home, too: the home of the Bear clan. Farewell, Orinha."

Their canoe moved out to meet Sorense and Tehagonra's in the middle of the river. They left for their village.

Father Ragueneau showed Radisson around the impressive fort. The fifty Frenchmen from the first expedition had built an impenetrable fortress in just a few months. A fifteen-foot-high palisade made out of broad tree trunks surrounded the buildings. The huge area inside that separated the enclosure from the homes was for the time being used only to farm pigs, sheltered as it was from thieves and wild animals, but dozens of people would be able to camp there. There would also be lots of room to store furs. Ladders led up to a parapet that ran along the enclosure, allowing the French to keep a watchful eye on the surrounding area and defend the fort if attacked. A projecting bastion reinforced each of the four corners. From there, the French would be able to shoot down at any attackers seeking shelter at the foot of the palisade or trying to set fire to it. Everything had been well thought out.

At the centre of the fort, two large wooden buildings were used for housing. The largest housed most of the men, and it was there that Radisson slept. The other building was used by the Jesuits and Commander Zacharie Dupuys. The kitchens, refectory, and goods warehouse were also there. In two separate cabins, a carpenter's workshop and a smithy rounded out the facilities. A small stone powder magazine, half buried in the ground and covered with a double roof, had been built in one corner.

Around the fort, all trees and shrubbery had been cut to the ground for two hundred paces to rule out the possibility of ambush. A few men had roughly ploughed the ground to sow wheat there. But the harvest was mediocre. The large vegetable garden promised better results. It was also here, outside the fort, that the French kept most of the pigs and all their chickens protected by a sturdy enclosure.

Of the seven Jesuit missionaries in Iroquois country, only Father Ragueneau and Father Le Moyne were currently living in the fort. The others had left on missions to various Onondaga villages. Most able-bodied men were busy putting the finishing touches to the French settlement; a severe fever epidemic had struck that summer and many were still getting back on their feet. The interpreter Guillaume Couture had decided to return to the colony with the weakest men, who had become a burden on everyone. Father Chaumonot was to go with them. Couture was currently at Onondaga with Commander Dupuys, where they had taken the Huron women.

CHAPTER 3

|||||||||||||||||||||||||||||||||||||||||||||||||||||||||||||||||||||||||||||||||||||||||

HARMONY

S INCE HIS ARRIVAL, Father Ragueneau had had many a conversation with his friend Simon Le Moyne about the mission. Father Frémin would go from village to village preaching
the good news with Father Le Mercier, who had even risked a
visit to the neighbouring Cayuga nation. Father Ménard and
Father Dablon had managed to settle permanently in two villages where there were chapels. In comparison, Ragueneau
was very disappointed with how they had been more or less
excluded from Onondaga, the nation's main village. Father Le
Moyne, whose domain it was, had close friends there and
regularly went to preach. But he hadn't wanted to confront his
allies when he was refused permission to settle there permanently and build a chapel in the village. Given the poor impression the French had made when they arrived in force the
previous year, he had decided it was best to be patient and
avoid further offending the Iroquois.

Ragueneau did not blame his friend. He decided, however,
that this conciliatory attitude had had its day. He was sure that
the Jesuits had to impose themselves at the very heart of the
nation, among the leading chiefs, if results were to match the
effort they had put into the mission.

To finalize their strategy, he called a meeting with Father Le Moyne, Commander Dupuys, and Radisson.

"Did they fully understand your message?" was the first question he asked Commander Dupuys. "After they massacred the Hurons who came with me, you were better placed than I to make sure they know there will be serious consequences if they mistreat the Huron women."

"I was firm," Dupuys replied. "Monsieur Couture told them we were keeping a close eye on them and that the French would be angry if they didn't keep their word. Fear not, Father. I made sure we will have their respect. I'm well used to it."

Although Dupuys was a military man, Radisson doubted his warning would have the desired effect. The commander spoke only a few words of Iroquois and didn't seem to have learned their rules of diplomacy. With his broad broad-feathered feathered hat and the sword he always carried around his waist, and his French-style clothes and large boots that were more fashionable than practical in this country, Radisson feared the Iroquois regarded him more as a scarecrow than a real threat.

"Now that our fort is finished," the commander added, "the Iroquois will have more respect for us. I will personally put more pressure on them, and leave them in no doubt that our weapons are superior. But you are right: the time has come for us to settle in Onondaga."

Radisson agreed with him on this point. It was true that the fort must have been intimidating for the Onondaga. Otherwise, the French would have been allowed to build it from the start.

"The Hurons' arrival has provided us with a fine pretext," added Ragueneau. "They are Christians and require religious guidance. Guidance that we will be able to provide if we are on site. We must seize this opportunity. They wanted the Hurons, and now they have them. Now we must show them what good Christians the women are, with priests to help them every day. What do you think, Simon?"

Father Le Moyne gave an unenthusiastic nod. Like Radisson, he preferred keeping a conciliatory attitude. But the chapel would have to be built one day, and now seemed like a good opportunity.

"Very well, Paul. We should try our luck."

Radisson let them discuss among themselves how best to present their plan to the Iroquois. Something else was on his mind. Before leaving, Guillaume Couture had told him he was beginning to question the attitude of many of the Iroquois. A great number of them were no more than tolerating the French, he said. They weren't really behind the alliance. Now that Couture had left with Father Chaumonot and the handful of sick men, Radisson was mulling over the consequences.

"It's all well and good having an impenetrable fort," he said, when everyone seemed to have had their say on the chapel. "But with no food reserves, the Iroquois will wear us down in the end. They can just let us die of hunger. We'll need to stock up for the winter, otherwise they'll have the upper hand."

Commander Dupuys, who had never before seriously considered the possibility of a long siege, was a little irked by Radisson's intervention. He had so little experience of the Iroquois' ambushes—their favourite tactic—that he had never reckoned on not being able to leave the fort to hunt and fish. But the provisions brought from Trois-Rivières, even along with the vegetables from the garden and the animals bred in the fort, wouldn't see them through the winter, leaving them well and truly vulnerable.

"Our food reserves are limited," he admitted.

"Until now," explained Father Le Moyne, "the Iroquois have been reluctant to share their best hunting grounds with us.

Fishing is all we have. Not to mention the fact that all our energy has gone into building the fort..."

"Then we must get started right away," Radisson insisted. Otherwise the Iroquois will be calling the shots, not us."

"Good point," said Ragueneau. "Take as many men as you need and make a start. Get everyone organized. We have plenty of time to make up for this. I'm counting on you, Radisson."

Father Le Moyne insisted on coming with Ragueneau and Radisson on their first visit to Onondaga. He was going to introduce them to Grand Chief Awenissera, his best friend and a staunch ally of the French. He would stay out of discussions, however. Ragueneau would lead and Father Le Moyne could intervene if his friend's requests did not go down well.

Out on the river that led to Onondaga, Ragueneau and Radisson discovered a magnificent land. Great old oak, elm, and walnut trees shaded the scattered undergrowth. Hazelnut trees were all around. Right by the village, vast, well-tended fields of corn, beans, and squash promised a bountiful harvest. The village itself was sizeable and surrounded by a double palisade. It reminded Radisson of the biggest Erie villages he had seen. From the front of the canoe, Father Le Moyne waved at the Iroquois looking on as they approached the village. Two of them rushed inside the enclosure to let their chiefs know a French canoe was on its way.

As Father Le Moyne and his companions stepped out of the canoe, Awenissera came to greet them with a few men and women dressed in leather and cloth. The old chief was still steady on his feet, although he moved slowly. The French waited for him to reach them and greeted him respectfully.

"Welcome home," Awenissera answered in Iroquois. His wrinkled face was aglow with heartfelt joy. Father Le Moyne introduced the newcomers.

"My friend Father Ragueneau, who has come to lend a hand, and Radisson, who has lived with the Mohawks."

"I hope our brothers treated you well," Awenissera said, knowing the hatred the Mohawks had for the French.

"They adopted me," Radisson replied. "I lived among them as a brother."

"I am glad of it."

In the clear blue sky, the September sun was still welcome. Awenissera led the visitors to the longhouse he lived in at the centre of the village. The thirty or so Iroquois who surrounded them all seemed happy to see them.

Radisson was struck by just how dense the village was. Twenty-odd longhouses stood side by side, taking up all available space inside the perimeter. If these longhouses held as many people as those in the Mohawk village where Radisson had lived, he reckoned, Onondaga's population was well over one thousand, maybe even two thousand. Trois-Rivières, Québec, and Montréal didn't have as many inhabitants. Sheaves of corn hung from the birch-bark walls, drying in the sun, but the bulk of the crop was still out in the fields.

Walking into the longhouse belonging to the Wolf clan, Radisson felt a wave of emotion wash over him. It was almost identical to the longhouse he had lived in. It was dark, quiet, and well equipped. The high roof got lost in the darkness, cluttered with goods and supplies. Triple bunk beds ran along the inclined walls on each side of the house. Ten fires were arranged in the middle of the central area, equal distance from each other and well aligned. Memories flooded Radisson's mind. He was happy and unhappy at once. Awenissera invited them to sit on the ground, around a fire in a stone circle.

Ragueneau began to speak. He announced that he wished to settle permanently in the village to take care of the Christian Hurons. The French also wanted a large amount of corn; they would trade French goods in return. Awenissera took a long while to react. He called on two men and an old woman to join them. Ragueneau repeated his request to them. The four Iroquois quickly agreed that this was too important an issue for the Wolf clan to deal with alone. Such decisions concerned the whole community. Awenissera told the Jesuit he would have to put his petitions before the village grand council, which he would convene the following day. In the meantime, he invited the guests to stay in his home.

The house was so quiet and Awenissera's welcome so warm that it reminded Radisson of the best days of his life in Iroquois country. After eating from a wooden bowl with no eating utensils, he was happy to lie down on the fur-covered bed he had been given for the night, lulled to sleep by murmured conversations from around the neighbouring fires. Everything was so peaceful here. Radisson slept as soundly as he did with his family in Trois-Rivières.

The next day, the village grand council met in a longhouse set aside for this very purpose. The central fire that burned there permanently symbolized the ties that had bound all Iroquois for generations. The councils of the Confederacy of the Five Nations, as well as councils involving all representatives of the Onondaga nation and those concerning the entire Onondaga village, were held here. It was an honour for the Frenchmen to be heard in such sacred surroundings.

Fifty men and women were gathered opposite Awenissera, Father Le Moyne, Ragueneau, and Radisson. Vincent Prudhomme, the young Frenchman who had arrived the previous year and had come with them, joined the Iroquois. He had quickly adapted to the customs of the country and already spoke fluent Iroquois. The elderly women taking part in the council were the clan mothers. The men were experienced war and peace chiefs. Radisson recognized Andoura among them, who had come to Trois-Rivières the previous winter. He was sitting in the front row, but never looked in Radisson's direction and Radisson had no way of indicating he wanted to talk to him. Radisson could see that he had lost a lot of weight.

The night before, the French had agreed that Ragueneau would first speak about religion, without an interpreter. Radisson would then talk about food supplies.

Awenissera began the discussions in his booming voice.

"I am happy to welcome among us a new Blackrobe who has come to help my friend Simon teach us more about the Great Spirit of the French. Those who have come with him are also welcome. You say this Great Spirit is all powerful, and it is our sincere desire to please him in order that we might benefit from his power. Our hearts and ears are open to your teaching. And we are gathered here today to listen to your request on this matter.

"Before it is your turn to speak, I want you to know that we share your pain and wish to help you heal your wound. The Hurons travelling with you were dear to your heart, we know. We are sorry they had to be killed, but I remind you that this decision is none of your concern. The conflict between the Huron and Iroquois nations existed long before the French settled on our shores. It is not for you to judge our actions. We did what was right in order to calm our spirits, who were angry with the Hurons. You must accept that. Just as we accepted that your people build a fort we consider to serve no purpose. Each to his customs.

"Now we must look to the future. The spirits of our ancestors are presently at peace and you have now settled among us to your satisfaction. The alliance between the Onondaga and the French will now be without clouds. It is up to us to make it more fruitful. I would like to reassure you that the Hurons we are welcoming among us are being treated like sisters we had lost and have now found. May your heart soon be at peace. Now speak, for we are listening."

Ragueneau stood to deliver his message. He had not understood everything, but had been touched by Awenissera's words about the death of the Hurons. With a discreet nod, Father Le Moyne indicated that he should not deviate from what they had agreed would be said. Ragueneau noted, however, that he would be able to use Awenissera's words to make his own even more convincing.

"I am glad to have arrived in your country," the Jesuit said in a firm, serious voice. "I have been waiting for this moment for a long time. As you said, I experienced great sadness on my way here, for I loved those Hurons as brothers. Your chiefs had already explained to me that their deaths will compensate the loss of those of you who were drowned when coming to fetch us. I will follow your advice and will not judge you for taking their lives. I respect your customs and am glad your spirits are now calm, despite the sorrow that I feel. Because even greater torment occupies my thoughts. Since I arrived in your country, I have felt the wrath of my God. I knew not why, until the answer came to me in a dream last night.

"Father Le Moyne told me that, despite your desire to open your hearts to the words of our Great Spirit and to please him, you have still not let him enter this village, the centre of your nation. No chapel has as yet been built here in Onondaga, and no missionaries are permitted to live here permanently. I now know that our Great Spirit is very angry because of your refusal to welcome him here and I fear he will seek revenge. He is very powerful, and I am fearful for you.

"To avoid a great misfortune befalling the Onondaga, I ask that you help me pacify our God. In my dream, I saw a wonderful chapel built in the midst of a bustling village, which I now recognize as your own. I lived permanently behind this chapel. I celebrated mass there every day before many Huron women and some Iroquois, too. Our God was pleased, and he smiled down on me. His anger was gone. Help me realize this dream and protect you from the wrath of our Great Spirit. I ask from the bottom of my heart that you grant me this favour, for the good of the Iroquois and the French, both of whom will profit from it. This is what I have to say to you."

Total silence fell on the assembly. No one had moved since Ragueneau had begun to speak. A mixture of surprise and fear was evident on the faces of the chiefs and the old women. Such a veiled threat had never been made by Father Le Moyne. Some Iroquois had been pleased with themselves for limiting the French influence in Onondaga, but this newcomer had sown serious doubt in their minds. They now knew that any reply to the Jesuit's requests would have grave consequences.

"As an act of our goodwill..." Ragueneau added, motioning for Radisson to open the large canvas sack he had brought with him, "...to show you that I seek only to spare you the wrath of our Great Spirit, I offer this gift to our friend Awenissera, who can share it among you at his convenience."

Radisson took six gleaming long-barrelled muskets from the bag, stacking them in a pyramid.

"These are the finest muskets the French have ever made. They have just arrived from the other side of the great salty sea. We have brought others with us to exchange with you later in return for furs. It is now time for Radisson to speak. He knows you well for he spent a long time among the Mohawks."

After Ragueneau had lowered expectations, it was now Radisson's turn to raise them. He gave those assembled a warm smile, making sure that he could be seen by all and delighted that it had fallen upon him to gratify the Iroquois and thank them for their welcome.

"The Onondaga have the finest country in all the world!" he began, looking several Iroquois in the eye. "Since I arrived a few days ago, your country has not ceased to amaze me! I have seen all kinds of game, and my French friends who have been living here for a year inform me that the fish are also plentiful. Your forests are full of nuts. Your woods allow you to make everything you need. What more could your people ask for? You already have everything we could ever dream of. My French friends and I are delighted to live with you in such a beautiful land, alongside such a generous people."

Radisson paused to see what impact his words were having. Faces were relaxing. Smiles were appearing.

"I also noticed how well kept your fields are. Your women are skilful and well used to growing corn, squash, and beans in a way the French have not yet mastered. We want you to show us how to have such fine harvests. You know that the French are also excellent farmers. But they lack experience in this new land. They planted French wheat around their fort without having the time to prepare the land, and now they are sorry because nothing grows better here than your wheat, your corn. We ask you to teach us how, the things you learned from your ancestors, so that we might enjoy such bountiful harvests ourselves. In the meantime, we are in need of your generosity.

"So that our union and the peace between us remain strong, so that trade makes us both more prosperous, we wish to exchange French goods in return for much corn and beans. Judging from what I have seen, your harvest will be plentiful and I have no fear of depriving you by asking you to share it with us. As you can see, we have precious goods to offer you in exchange, such as these muskets and a great deal of powder. Beautiful sheaves of corn hanging from the walls of your homes have already caught my eye, while countless ears of corn are still to be harvested in your fields. We are asking you for one hundred large baskets of corn and twenty baskets of beans, once they are dry and are ready to be stored.

"We make this request because we had to leave much food behind along the way, as our Iroquois guides have surely told you already. Even though we anticipated every eventuality, our cautious guides insisted we could not bring everything with us. Their thinking was perhaps well founded, but today we find ourselves penalized. We French showed much bravery and would have brought everything along to be sure of never going hungry. We hope you will agree to make up for the caution they showed. If you agree to my request, all the French will be grateful to you. Father Ragueneau, Father Le Moyne, and I can promise you that."

To the surprise of the two Jesuits, who had not known how Radisson planned to close his speech, the young man suddenly produced a fistful of iron needles and fish hooks from the small bag he was carrying over his shoulder.

"I, too, have gifts for you," he exclaimed. "It is not much, but I offer them gladly."

Radisson began to walk around the assembly, placing in each outstretched hand a few hooks or needles from his personal supply of trading goods, starting with Chief Awenissera. He went from person to person until there were no more gifts left. He gave some to Andoura, who did not appear to recognize him. Radisson was so taken aback that he couldn't think quickly enough to let him know he wanted to speak to him. All the Iroquois were either delighted or amused. They had found their good humour, even though they had not forgotten the important decision they would have to make regarding the Great Spirit of the French. The issue of food supplies would also have to be carefully considered: the well-being of the whole community was at stake.

Awenissera closed the assembly by promising the Jesuit his request would be discussed in the very near future in each longhouse and would soon be a matter for discussion at the next village council. They would have to wait until the whole harvest had been gathered before looking into how much corn could be given to the French. As soon as both decisions had been made, a messenger would send for the French.

Radisson let Prudhomme and the two Jesuits return to the French fort alone; he still had business to take care of in Onondaga. He wanted to meet Andoura, who had slipped out immediately after the council, to find out why none of the emissaries they had met in Trois-Rivières had come to see them in Montréal. He also hoped to get Ononta and Mahatari's permission to go to the Bear clan's hunting grounds.

Entering one of the two homes that the clan's many members lived in, Radisson came face to face with Ononta. His head, shoulders, and back were covered in wolfskin. He was holding a turtle shell rattle in one hand, a small round drum in the other, and wearing a bag decorated with porcupine quills around his neck. The Iroquois stood stock-still before Radisson, who was astounded to see him dressed like this.

"Go see Mahatari," the Iroquois told him after a moment. "She has something for you."

Ononta continued on, disappearing into the neighbouring house while Radisson made his way hesitantly into the darkness, spotting Mahatari some distance away. She and her husband lived at this end of the longhouse, in an area half closed off by a wall of intertwined branches, the likes of which Radisson had never seen before in a longhouse.

"Hello, Orinha," said Mahatari, moving toward him.

Radisson was gradually getting used to the couple calling him by his former Iroquois name.

"I just bumped into your husband... Why is he so dressed up?"

"Take a seat," she replied.

Radisson recalled the respect Ononta had been shown on their travels and the eagle he had taken down with one shot. Mahatari sat beside him, close to the almost extinguished fire, without saying a word. He took the wooden cup of water she handed him and drank slowly. Further away, lots of plants were being hung to dry upside down. Radisson was beginning to understand. He repeated his question.

"He has gone to heal a sick woman," she replied.

"He's a shaman, isn't he?"

"Yes."

Suddenly everything was clear. That's why a small, scrawny man who barely said a word was so respected. No one knew when they might need him to calm a spirit, tell them what the future had in store, or explain a dream. More than anything, no one wanted him to one day use his power against them. But Radisson could not understand why Ononta seemed to have taken him under his wing.

"He knew your father," Mahatari explained. "Garagonké came to our village a few days after meeting you for the first time. He had come to get our village to rise up against the French. But he spoke very well of you. He was proud that you were joining his family to replace one of his beloved sons. Ononta is pleased you honoured him by fighting the Erie. Your father was a great warrior."

"I know."

Radisson was itching to ask a question. Although he was almost certain what the reply would be, he wanted to ask it just the same to eliminate all doubt from his mind.

"Garagonké is dead, isn't he?"

"Yes. The Algonquins killed your father in an ambush. He didn't stand a chance."

The ties between his old adoptive family and the shaman, not to mention Mahatari's concern for him and confirmation that his Iroquois father was indeed dead, plunged Radisson into a state of uncertainty. This past life he had so enjoyed was well and truly over. He did not regret running away from his village, even though he was once again among the Iroquois. Had it not been for Ragueneau and his mission, were it not for the fur trade grinding to a halt, he would probably never have set foot in their country again, except perhaps to meet with a shaman. And now he had unwittingly met a shaman who knew him through someone else. It was more than he could have hoped for.

"Ononta said you had something for me."

"Wait here."

Mahatari walked over to where the plants were hanging. She and her husband did not dress in cloth like so many other Indians. Instead, they dressed from head to toe in leather, as they had done in the days before the white men had arrived. She took down three long feathers hanging among the plants and gave them to Radisson.

"These are feathers from the eagle Ononta killed when you were scared you were going to die. He hopes they will open your eyes. You were so afraid that you did not understand this spirit was watching over you. It was there. It came to reassure you. Ononta could see it, but you did not. He had to sacrifice it to show you. This is a very precious gift he has given you. Take good care of it."

Holding the feathers, Radisson could feel the same warmth pulsing through him as when he picked up his knife. He instinctively gripped its handle without taking it out of its sheath. Energy coursed through his body. He felt as though he was about to fly away. Mahatari could see his reaction.

"You see? The eagle is speaking to you. He's watching over you. You need not worry. It's a very powerful spirit."

Radisson was a little irritated by the veiled criticisms Ononta was making by giving him this present.

"How could I have known the eagle spirit was protecting me? No one ever taught me these things. The French don't think like that and my Mohawk brothers never mentioned a thing. I need Ononta to do more for me than give me feathers. I need him to teach me."

Mahatari stayed calm.

"I need him to explain how I can communicate with the eagle, how it can give me strength. I don't know what to do with these feathers. How do you want the gift to be useful to me? Ononta must show me. He must tell me why I am so attached to this knife and why the eagle is the spirit I must revere."

Mahatari thought for a moment.

"You will sleep here. Tomorrow, you can talk to Ononta. Perhaps he will agree to show you the secrets you want to know."

Radisson had forgotten all about the hunting grounds that had brought him there. Supplies for the French fort no longer seemed so important. He had a date with destiny.

All night long, Ononta called on the spirits by singing, chanting, and beating on his drum, in the hope of saving the dying woman. In vain. She died in the early hours of the morning. The shaman came home tired and frustrated. He slept for a few hours and ate in silence with Radisson and Mahatari. His wife tried to talk him into teaching the young Frenchman. He refused: custom had it that everything to do with each person's totemic animal had to remain a secret. Radisson brandished the eagle fathers in front of the Iroquois. He implored him to reveal his connection to the eagle, but to no avail. Ononta remained stony-faced.

"I couldn't care less if the eagle is my animal!" Radisson exploded. "Your secrets are worthless! The Iroquois have nothing to teach me!"

He flung the feathers to the ground and whirled away from the shaman.

Ononta knew that the eagle would prove a valuable guide to the adopted Frenchman, an ally like no other, to give his life meaning and direction. He weighed up the importance of the precious gifts the spirits had given him. In a way, he regretted not revealing all to Radisson, since it was within his powers to teach the young man and rid him of the uncertainties that were preventing his talents from blossoming. When he really thought about it, he considered Radisson something of an exception: not quite French, not quite Iroquois. Why not make an exception for him, too? He walked off for a while to think the situation over.

"Very well. I will teach you what you want to know. But first we will wait for night to fall so that no one sees us together."

The two men withdrew to a teepee deep in the woods. Ononta would spend whole days fasting there, preparing plant-based remedies and consulting the spirits. Mahatari, who also knew a lot of secrets, never ventured there. Around the teepee, other small bark cabins were used for other ceremonies, healing the sick, and interpreting omens. By comparison, Ononta would have an easy time of things today. All he had to do was speak to the young man.

With the help of scared herbs, he first had to purify and cleanse the teepee of all interference from the spirits. Radisson/ Orinha was behaving admirably. He stayed calm and listened as the shaman told him what to do. He was ready to receive his teaching. Ononta hoped that this experience with a Frenchman would help him deal with the situation his people were now facing as the Jesuits preached all over the land about the power of their Great Spirit and disparaged the Iroquois spirits.

Radisson, meanwhile, had been hoping for a long time to understand the enigmatic powers his knife held over him. The eagle was apparently his totemic animal. But what did that even mean? What relationship would he have to develop with the bird? What meaning, what importance would he have to give to this relationship? He kept a close eye on Ononta and did all he asked of him. He quickly grew used to the animal skulls on fur pelts nearby, to the tangle of plants and feathers hanging everywhere, to the animal skins, and to the masks dangling from sticks of different lengths beaten down into the ground. He was not afraid of Ononta casting an evil spell on him.

The shaman had stopped tending to the fire. To better communicate with the spirit of the eagle, he wore a headdress of eagle feathers long enough to reach his shoulders, a head and beak attached to his forehead. They were both sweating from the heat of the tent, even though they were bare chested. Smoke began to escape from the top of the teepee. It no longer stung Radisson's eyes. They sat cross-legged facing each other on either side of the fire. Ononta threw a few more handfuls of tobacco, sage, and sweetgrass onto it. Radisson was holding the three feathers the shaman had given him in one hand, the handle of his eagle-head knife in the other.

"How did this knife come into your possession?" Ononta asked him.

"It was in a house in a Dutch village surrounding Fort Orange. I was there trading with my brother Ganaha two years ago. A young Dutch woman had been using it to chop vegetables. It was lying on a table. As soon as I saw it, I had to have it. Once it was in my hand, I felt a great surge of energy run through me. I could no longer let go."

Ononta nodded. All the signs were in agreement. His intuition had been right. His teaching could begin.

"Your knife is not the source of this energy," he said. "You are contacting the spirit of the eagle through the knife. The eagle is your totemic animal. It is calling out to you. You must answer."

"What can I do?"

"You have lived long enough among us to know that the spirits give life to everything. But you did not learn to listen to them as attentively as you must. You do not know how to make allies. The spirit of the eagle is calling you with all its might. This is an opportunity for you: it is calling out to you like this because you have its qualities, exceptional qualities that you have not yet learned to develop. The eagle is your brother. You must listen to it, follow it, honour it. It will help you grow. It will guide you."

"What is it telling me? Where is it taking me?"

Ononta tried to calm the young man who was in such a hurry.

"The eagle flies so high," the shaman continued, "that sometimes it disappears behind the clouds. It reaches the sun. At the same time, it feeds on animals on this earth. It belongs to both worlds. It lives in the sky and on the ground. It is the bridge between humankind and the spirits, between dreams and reality. It is like you: you are half-Iroquois, half-Frenchman. The eagle teaches us that all is linked, that we depend on each other, like the sun allows seeds planted in the soil to grow."

Radisson could now see what the eagle could bring him. He had one hundred questions. But Ononta wanted him to stay quiet. He still had much to say about the animal his people venerated. Radisson understood that he must listen to him.

"When the eagle soars so high that we lose sight of it, it flies off in all directions. It flies over obstacles that blind us. If you look with your eyes, the eagle will show you what you cannot see today. You will learn how to see in every direction, to make out what others do not see. From such a great height, it swoops down low to capture the hare or salmon that did not see it. It is the ultimate hunter. It strikes like lightning. It is as powerful as thunder. Admire it. Honour it. If you draw inspiration from its superior powers, the eagle will teach you the power of the warrior and the perceptiveness of the sage. The feathers I gave you will help you reach out to it. Its spirit is giving you the energy you can feel. If you are receptive to it, if you watch closely, you will be able to acquire its qualities. These feathers are light and fragile and yet they are powerful. They enable the eagle to fly faster and higher than any other animal. They enable it to strike at the best moment, from the best angle. They will help you acquire these qualities."

Carried away by the admiration he felt for the master of the skies, Ononta caught his breath for a moment. He threw some more tobacco onto the fire. The night was dark and quiet. Radisson was hanging on the shaman's every word, fascinated by his teaching.

"The eagle is a brother to the sun. It soars amidst the spirits. But just as the sun can heat or burn, its power can do good or ill. Be careful with the powerful spirit within you. Be in no doubt: the eagle is your totemic spirit. It is calling out to you. It has adopted you. If you take the time to understand its true nature, if you are inspired by its greatness, you will soar just as high as the eagle. You will be as magnanimous as the greatest of chiefs. You will find the means to realize your dreams. You will discover how to adapt to the sky every bit as much as to the earth. The spirit of the eagle will teach you to transform yourself. You will be able to soar to see in all directions or swoop down upon your prey as needed. The eagle will protect you like no other because it is a powerful spirit. No bird dares threaten it in the sky. On the ground, no animal dares touch it. Awaken its power within you and you will grow more than you could ever imagine."

Radisson was shocked. This shaman was painting such a fabulous picture of his destiny! He hardly dared believe it. And yet, the feathers and his knife were pulsating right there in his hand. The spirit of the eagle was filling his body with a powerful energy. He felt free of all constraints—cleansed, purified, renewed. And for the very first time, he understood the meaning and significance of the energy coursing through him.

"I have something else to teach you," Ononta added. "The ties that bind each of us to our totemic animals are a secret because they are unique. There are a number of eagles, and all the qualities of all the eagles will not be within your reach. Some hunt animals on the ground, others fish, while others steal their food. You must decide which of all these qualities will be of greatest use to you. You must also cast off the weights that are dragging you down. You must make yourself as light as a bird. With each passing day, with every dive, the eagle perseveres. The energy that sustains it is renewed. You must never allow yourself to become discouraged."

Ononta fell silent. Radisson's head was spinning. He had sensed all this in the courage shown by his father Garagonké, in the wisdom of his war chief Kondiaronk, in the way his brother Ganaha hunted. But never had he come into contact with the foundation of their inner lives. He had not known what lay behind their strength. And now Ononta had given him this unexpected gift.

Looking back over all the shaman had revealed to him, Radisson realized he had far to go as an apprentice. But he had just taken a decisive step, as though walking out of a dark forest into the light.

Radisson led one of the canoes speeding toward the French fort. Ononta and Mahatari's son Denongea paddled the heavy canoe up onto the shore. Five Iroquois from the Bear clan followed closely behind. They brought with them five dead deer, three bears, and six beavers.

"What a haul!" cried the Frenchmen who had come to greet them. "God is great! The hunt was a success!"

Father Ragueneau rushed up to them as they were loading the meat onto the makeshift cart that rattled its way back and forth between the river and the fort.

"What happened to you?" he asked. "I've been terribly worried about you!"

"Out hunting, Father. Out hunting, as you can see. It took longer than expected, but I got what I was after. I can even go back any time I want. I got permission from the Bear clan to hunt on the best grounds along with them and two or three of our own men."

"Very well, but you will have to wait for a day or two. A messenger just brought me word that the Iroquois have agreed to our requests! Now I must go to the village to decide where the chapel should go and oversee its construction. The corn you asked for will soon be ready, too. But this time you're staying with me. I've had enough fretting for one day."

CHAPTER 4

THE OTHER SIDE OF THE COIN

A CCOMPANIED BY THREE CHIEFS from the Bear clan, Awenissera showed Father Ragueneau the two sites they were proposing for the chapel to be built on. The chiefs' favourite was outside the palisade by the entrance gate. There, it would be seen by all in the vicinity. They suggested putting up a small enclosure on two or three sides, whichever the Jesuit preferred. Ragueneau was not satisfied. They led him on to the only other space still available inside the village of Onondaga, tucked away in a corner. The Jesuit wasn't any more taken with the idea.

"Why not in front of the council house?" he asked.

"You chapel will be in the way there and it will be too small," Awenissera answered. "There is no room."

"Let's go take a look all the same," Ragueneau urged.

The chiefs went with him reluctantly. At best, they would be able to build a small bark chapel there. But it would obstruct the entrance to the council house. Even Father Ragueneau, who dreamt of occupying such a central position, could see the problem. Radisson was relieved to see his master's hesitation because here the chapel would be vying for importance with what was a sacred place for their Confederacy. This was no way to improve relations with the Iroquois. Ragueneau did not insist. And so the group returned to the second site.

"Here it shall be," the Jesuit declared after some reflection. "I am anxious that our chapel be in the village among you. We will place a high cross on top so that everyone will know where to find it."

The chiefs agreed. Construction would begin the following day.

"Until the chapel is ready, you will stay with my family," Awenissera told them.

The next day, while Ragueneau traced the chapel's perimeter and fifteen Iroquois gathered the wood and bark they would need to build it, Radisson inquired about the corn that was to be sent to the French. Awenissera's wife and other women from the Bear clan had started shelling the dried ears of corn and were collecting the grains in large wicker baskets. Fifteen or so were already full. The rest would be ready in a day or two.

In the meantime, Radisson went for a walk through the village. He tried to put Ononta's advice into practice. He looked at the activity surrounding him with the eyes of an eagle, as though he were soaring through the air.

Getting the harvest ready and preparing for winter was keeping a lot of people busy. Sheaves of corn hung from the walls of every home. The harvest had been a good one. Inside, women shelled beans, too. Others were out bringing in squash from the fields, while men repaired bark roofs or smoked fish. Many headed to the woods to hunt or gather firewood.

Radisson noticed the rather cool reception he was getting. Few Iroquois smiled at him or bothered to greet him. He felt like an outsider. Only members of the Wolf clan were truly thoughtful and welcoming toward him and the other Frenchmen. Even Mahatari and Ononta were only kind to him because he was part Iroquois.

Suddenly he saw Andoura walk between two longhouses. Radisson darted around the building the Iroquois had disappeared behind and found himself face to face with him. This time, Andoura could not slip away.

"Hello!" said Radisson, flashing him his best smile. "I'm happy to see you again."

The chief was embarrassed and pretended not to recognize him. He tried to step around Radisson, but the Frenchman stood in his path and drew his knife, planting its handle right under Andoura's nose. The Iroquois gave a start, and his hand was instinctively drawn to his own knife.

"Incredible, isn't it?"

The Iroquois did not reply. His eyes were wide with surprise. Radisson felt the need to refresh his memory.

"I thought the very same thing when you took out your knife in Trois-Rivières last winter. I was there. Don't you remember? I'll never forget it."

Andoura had neither the presence nor the assurance he had shown in Trois-Rivières. After a long moment's hesitation, looking Radisson square in the eye as though to read his intentions, he took out his knife and laid it in his hands to compare the two. The likeness was uncanny. The handle was identical: there was the same slender eagle head, the same hooked beak, the same beady eyes, the same broad feathers that went all the way down to the blade, opening out ever so slightly. They had surely been made by the same person. How else could they be so similar? Only the blades were slightly different. And yet Andoura's knife had been made especially for him in extraordinary circumstances. He would have sworn that it was one of a kind.

"Where did you get this knife?" the chief demanded.

"At Fort Orange, in a Dutchman's house. And you?"

"I can't tell you here."

They were still examining their knives. Then their eyes met again with a fiery, knowing look.

"I am sorry my brothers killed the Hurons," said Andoura. "I was against it."

Surprised by this unexpected admission, Radisson didn't know what to say.

"I must speak with you," the Iroquois added. "It's important. Join me tonight in the council house when the moon has set. And be careful. We can't let anybody see us."

"I'll be there."

The Iroquois was gone in a flash.

Father Ragueneau had been sleeping for a long time. Exhausted but happy to have helped put up the long poles that made up the chapel's frame, he was constantly thanking Awenissera for welcoming him into his house while the chapel was being built. He was tired but excited. By now, everyone else in the longhouse was asleep. Only Radisson was still awake, afraid of missing his rendezvous. The night seemed to drag on forever.

So as not to fall asleep, Radisson sat on his bed, trying to determine the hour and the position of the moon. He thought back to his dream in Trois-Rivières once the Iroquois ambassadors had gone. His father Garagonké had told him: "Take this knife, my son, and be brave, for the lives of the Frenchmen are in your hands." He had not spent long trying to work out what the dream might mean, but he should have because today the words still troubled him. He clutched his knife in both hands and closed his eyes. He opened them again to ease the transition from dreams to reality. He closed them, then opened them again. But it was all still as much of a mystery as ever.

The moon had probably set by now. They must not be surprised by the first light. Radisson stood up very carefully, anxious not to wake a soul, and tiptoed to the end of the house. The walk had never seemed so long. Nobody could see him. At last, he lifted the bark flap and found himself outside. Clouds masked part of the sky. The moon, hidden by the neighbouring house, would soon drop off the horizon. It was time.

Radisson found his way around the village as best he could. He recognized the small council house and risked lifting the bark flap. He hoped that Andoura had kept his word. It was pitch-black inside, apart from a pile of embers in the sacred fire, which glowed red without emitting any real light. He groped his way along.

"Andoura?" he whispered. "Are you there?"

"Radisson? Is that you?"

"Yes, it's me. Where are you?"

The Frenchman stopped as he felt the Iroquois' breath against his face. Andoura touched him with his fingertips. Recognizing his bushy beard, he began to speak in a low voice.

"We don't have much time. First, you should know that two of the three chiefs who came with me to Trois-Rivières are dead. I myself was gravely ill. The fourth, who was against the alliance with the French, has remained in good health."

Radisson was distressed to hear this: a stroke of bad luck had surely left a very bad impression.

"Many took it to be a bad omen and have become suspicious of the French. Some are no longer in favour of peace. Until now, chiefs like Awenissera and I had the upper hand, but things are changing. The chapel has left many furious. Awenissera is clever. He spoke well and managed to convince a majority of chiefs that it was time to let the Blackrobes live in our village. But those who were against it held a secret council. Awenissera is to be frozen out. I was invited to speak of what happened in Trois-Rivières. The chiefs opposed to the alliance want to know if the French cast an evil spell on us."

"The French never cast evil spells," Radisson replied. "They want peace. For the good of your people, and for the good of mine."

"I will speak again in favour of the alliance with the French," Andoura reassured him. "But I have learned that a Mohawk chief will also speak. Almost all the Mohawks are against you. He will surely urge us to pick up our weapons and join forces with them. Because of them the Hurons travelling with you were killed. They convinced our war chiefs that the Hurons are our enemies and that we should be done with the men who betrayed our ancestors to adopt the Great Spirit of the white men. There were long discussions before the expedition set out. That's why it arrived so late in Montréal. That's why I did not go. I was against the plan."

It was so dark and Andoura's words were so troubling that Radisson wondered if he was dreaming. It surprised him to learn the peace was so fragile, in spite of Pierre Godefroy's warnings and the many times the Iroquois had changed their minds. Two camps of Iroquois were well and truly facing off against each other. One respected the commitments they had made to the French; the other was plotting to have them overturned.

"Is Awenissera really with us?"

"Yes. He is your most faithful ally. But many young war chiefs are muttering behind his back that he is too old to grasp what is happening to us. People are turning their backs on our traditions. Our country is in uproar. Illnesses we do not know are decimating our people. The young people say we must fight back against our invaders. But Awenissera and I believe we must ally ourselves with the French in spite of the risks, and profit from your strength. We have our supporters, but our numbers are dwindling."

"You must stay with us, Andoura. You are in the right. We want to trade with the Iroquois. We want them to know our Great Spirit and share his power with you. We want to help you, Andoura."

"I always speak in favour of peace. That is my path. Because it is tied to my knife and because you too are for peace, I will one day tell you how I learned to take that path. The same destiny binds us."

"It's true that I am for peace and that our knives seem to be nudging us in this direction, even though it is hard to understand."

They both silently considered the impossible coincidence that bound them and pondered what they could do to avoid war again.

Radisson knew Father Ragueneau well enough to be sure the Jesuits had no ill intentions. He also knew the powers of the French were not as great as the Iroquois supposed. But how could they be convinced?

"Listen," said Radisson. "Our knives confirm that we are allies. We must work together to save the peace. After the secret council, I will come to your house to trade and you can tell me what was said. You must let me know what's happening. That's the best way to safeguard the peace. The French and the Iroquois can get along. We just need to put up a bit of a struggle to get there."

"Very well. But we must act in secret. If it gets back to the partisans of war that I am talking to the French, they will keep me away from the meetings, as they did with Awenissera."

"You can count on me. They won't suspect a thing. Now it's time to go our separate ways."

"May the spirit of the eagle be with you."

Radisson saw Andoura again a few days later in the house of the Turtle clan. When Andoura introduced him to his daughter Lavionkié, who was Radisson's age, the Frenchman was at a loss for words. He had never seen such a beautiful Iroquois woman. She had big hazel eyes, soft and bright like a doe's. She wore her long black hair in braids, accentuating the glow of her face. And her slender leather dress enhanced her graceful body. She rummaged around in the package Radisson had just placed on the ground, curious to see all that he had brought with him. She was overcome with delight when she discovered a long piece of cloth, knife blades, and iron scrapers. Radisson could barely tear his gaze away from the girl long enough to speak with her father.

"I brought along some of the goods we have here, but there is much more back at the French fort."

Andoura grinned broadly. He could see that his daughter had caught Radisson's eye. So much the better. The young Frenchman shared part of his destiny. He was a likeable character and his attraction to his daughter would provide a cover for them exchanging information.

"Be seated," Andoura told him. "Let's talk. I have a few beaver pelts in reserve."

Ogienda, Andoura's wife, moved back a fair distance, but Lavionkié stayed by Radisson's side. She stared at him intently, not the least embarrassed. The Frenchman couldn't help but admire her and return her smiles. The negotiation with Andoura did not take long: the cloth, a scraper, and two knives were exchanged in return for two beaver pelts. Radisson threw in a handful of sewing needles.

"Your mother needs you, Lavionkié," said her father so that he and Radisson could be alone.

The two men walked to one end of the longhouse. After making sure that no one could hear them, a serious-looking Andoura summed up in a low voice the decisions that had been made the previous night.

"Another secret council is to be held on the night of the next new moon. Cayuga and Seneca chiefs will join us. They are all opposed to the alliance with the French. The two Mohawk chiefs who were there yesterday are to return with a Huron who will tell us how the Frenchmen ruined their country. I will take part in the council and shall again speak up for the French. The chiefs thought it best that someone in favour of the alliance be heard to better put things in perspective. But those in favour of war are gaining ground."

Radisson listened, his head low. Instinctively, he turned to see Lavionkié waving over at him. She had kept her eyes trained on him and had been waiting for him to look up. Radisson was deeply troubled. He gave her a half-smile. Even though he was happy that the dazzling young woman liked him, the news he had just learned was very worrying indeed. Once he was back outside, he didn't know what to feel. The situation was too serious not to warn Father Ragueneau right away. He hoped the Jesuit would react calmly—and keep the secret to himself. At any rate, together they would have a better idea of what to do next. Radisson met him at the site where the chapel was being built.

"Can you come with me for a moment, Father? I have something to tell you."

Ragueneau could see Radisson's concern right away. Without a moment's hesitation, he followed him outside the village to river's edge so they could be completely alone.

"I have just been told a secret, Father. A number of chiefs met last night. They intend to break the peace."

"Are you sure?"

"Certain. These chiefs were responsible for killing the Hurons. They are conspiring against us. Andoura told me, and he's firmly on our side. But we must keep the whole thing a secret if we want to continue counting on him."

The Jesuit swallowed his anger. The situation reminded him of his final years among the Hurons just before everything unravelled. Two clans had formed: one for and one against the French. He knew from experience that they would need to tread carefully from now on.

"This is very serious indeed," he concluded. "You were right to warn me. But there's no point panicking. First, we will try to verify what you have learned, as discreetly as possible. If it's only a few desperados we're dealing with, we'll find a way to deal with them. But if a real storm is brewing, we'll have to find a way out of this predicament."

To start with, Ragueneau suggested no one other than the Jesuit missionaries be warned. Radisson would first advise Father Le Moyne back at the fort. Father Le Moyne would then travel the country to ask the four other priests on the mission for more information. He would ask them in a roundabout way, without hinting that they had gotten wind of a plot being hatched. Radisson would be able to protect his precious source. They would know more within a moon or two.

"We'll inform everyone after that," concluded Ragueneau. "Now go. Bring this corn back to the fort as quickly as you can. We need it very much. I'll take care of finishing the chapel while you talk to Father Le Moyne. Nice work, Radisson. Now don't breathe a word of this to anyone!"

Before leaving the village with the others carrying the corn, Radisson passed by the Bear longhouse to see Ononta and Mahatari. Perhaps he might learn something there. He was in such a hurry that he walked right in. Mahatari was alone.

Radisson could immediately sense that he was interrupting something.

"I'm here to speak with Ononta."

Mahatari took a while to answer.

"Hello, Orinha."

She did not even turn around.

"Is he here?"

"No. He's at his cabin. You mustn't disturb him."

Radisson was taken aback at her brusqueness.

"OK then. I'll come back later."

Mahatari was grinding plants in a small mortar. He walked over to her.

"I hope I'm not disturbing you."

She did not answer, a sure sign that he was.

"You said I would always be welcome here."

"You are. But some days less than others."

"How come?"

At last she made an effort to smile at him. Then she picked up her work where she had left off without saying a word. Radisson stayed by her side until she gave in and spoke to him.

"Ononta is annoyed that the French sorcerer is moving into the village to take his place."

Radisson couldn't contradict her. Ragueneau and the other Jesuits were doing all they could to discredit the Iroquois shamans.

"That's nothing to do with me," he replied. "Anyway, your council authorized it."

"I know. But you're often with him."

"He needs me because I know the Iroquois well. I'm trying to help him understand you. It's not easy. I came to ask Ononta if I could stay here for a while. I don't want to stay with Ragueneau in the small home they're building for him behind his chapel. I feel much more at home here."

"You can come visit me from time to time, but you can't sleep here any longer. Ononta is too angry."

The threat was clearer now. Radisson was losing a guide, and the French had another enemy.

"I'll go sleep at Andoura's house then. I don't want to be with Father Ragueneau all the time. I'm not like him. Look at me: I'm wearing one of the feathers Ononta gave me."

"I know. I felt it when you came in."

Radisson was no longer surprised at how much she was able to divine. She and her husband had special powers.

"Go on," she said. "They're waiting for you. You'd better leave if you want to reach the fort before nightfall."

"I'll come back and see you, Mahatari."

"My door will never be closed, Orinha. But going to stay with Andoura is a good idea. Your heart will find love there. Now go. And be careful."

The slaves and the Huron women made up the convoy carrying eighty-seven large baskets of corn and ten of beans. Radisson walked at the front with two heavily armed Iroquois warriors. The rest followed behind in single file on the path that led from the village to the fort. Some twenty more armed warriors mounted guard at regular intervals and brought up the rear. Because no one would dare steal the corn right in the heart of Onondaga country, it seemed as though the men and women carrying the baskets were prisoners and the warriors were there to ensure they did not escape.

The group arrived at the fort a little before sunset. Commander Dupuys, who had been sent word the day before, had hastily ordered tents to be put up inside the enclosure so that everyone could be given something to eat along with a bed for the night. The Iroquois took the opportunity to give a handful of old muskets to the gunsmith and to take back others that he had repaired.

That evening, after Father Le Moyne had blessed and comforted the Huron women, Radisson went off with him to the Jesuits' apartment. Outside, the fires lit by the Iroquois and Hurons burned so brightly that there was no need for candles: they could see each other in the light filtering in through the windows. Radisson made sure they were as discreet as possible so as not to arouse the suspicions of Commander Dupuys or other Frenchmen. Father Le Moyne had never met Radisson in private before.

"Things are looking bad, Father Le Moyne," Radisson told him. "I have learned that the Iroquois want to break the peace."

He had expected a sign of despondency from the Jesuit, but Father Le Moyne remained quiet and impassive. Radisson explained to him that opponents of the alliance with the French had made their voices heard as soon as the emissaries returned from Trois-Rivières that previous winter. Those who wanted to kill the Hurons had gained the upper hand. Now building the chapel had angered them.

Simon Le Moyne listened reverently. He knew the young man was close to the Iroquois and that his information was reliable. He feared the Huron scenario was about to repeat itself.

"They held a secret council several days ago and another is planned for the next new moon. Mohawks, Cayuga, and Seneca will be taking part. Hurons are also coming to tell them how the French destroyed their country. The war camp is still growing, Father. It's very worrying."

Simon Le Moyne nodded. He was an optimist by nature and had often been gladdened by the great progress made since the first day when the Iroquois welcomed him to Onondaga, but the cold reception some chiefs continued to reserve for them left him fearing that an abrupt change of mind was still possible.

Radisson told him that Ragueneau wanted to make only the Jesuits aware of the situation; he was counting on them to investigate and see just how far rumblings of discontent had spread. He wanted Father Le Moyne to leave immediately and bring them the news.

"I will leave tomorrow," said Le Moyne. "I will also be sure to encourage and reward our allies. It is thanks to them that we are so well settled today. And it is perhaps they who will have the last word. Let's not lose heart."

"Andoura will speak up for us at the next council. We can count on him."

"We have others on our side throughout this land. I will be sure to leave them a gift or two as I travel around. You will also need to recruit more sources. I know a hateful man who strikes me as a good candidate. His name is Ouatsouan. He's a brother of Awenissera and he is incredibly jealous of his influence. He speaks ill of everyone behind their backs and fawns over them when they're near. He is bound to be in favour of war, if only to oppose his brother, but he is so greedy he should be easy to bribe. He knows absolutely everything; he wriggles his way in everywhere like a grass snake. You will have to be careful, naturally, but if you name your price, he will tell you the truth."

"We will have to step up trade to hide what we're up to."

"Indeed. That is a good thing, in any case. The Iroquois are often complaining that we don't have enough goods to offer them. That can only help our cause. Speaking of which, weren't we supposed to give them a vast amount of powder in exchange for the corn?"

"That's what was agreed."

"Nothing could please them more. If God breathed fire like a cannon, if he had swords for arms, if his body were a giant roll of cloth, they would all have converted a long time ago! Unfortunately, what we're offering them is rather less concrete; we're going to have to be patient if we are to lead them along the path of faith."

Father Le Moyne was again lost in his thoughts. The light from the distant fires danced across his face, giving him a dramatic look.

"Let's just hope they don't use this powder to kill us..."

Only the stars lit up the cool night. A handful of chiefs from the Onondaga, Mohawks, Cayuga, and Seneca, wrapped up in their wool blankets, made their way discreetly to the Bear clan house. They walked in one by one for their secret meeting. The Iroquois were still trying to regain their balance after years of uninterrupted disruption. The Frenchmen arriving among them had only heightened the tension.

Takanissorens, the Onondaga chief chairing the council, believed it was time for the discontent felt by many to reach the ears of those in favour of the alliance with the French. They had to face facts: their dominance was now being contested.

Takanissorens asked Andoura to speak first since the decisions to be made would have serious consequences and the position that had prevailed for the past two years should be heard. Andoura reminded them that the French had given the Onondaga all the goods they desired. They repaired their muskets and respected their customs, as the Iroquois had wished. They kept their promises and counterbalanced the Dutch, who had given so much to the Mohawks.

"Why turn our backs on them now?" Andoura asked. "Because they want us to know the Great Spirit who makes them so powerful?"

One of the two Hurons present was bursting with impatience as he listened.

"Don't you see their Great Spirit is malevolent? He'll bring about your downfall just like he did ours," he exclaimed as soon as Andoura had finished. "The Blackrobes have only one thing in mind: they want to destroy the Iroquois just like they destroyed the Hurons! Kill them or send them packing before it's too late!"

"Tonneraont should wait until it's his turn to speak," Takanissorens intervened. "Does Andoura have anything to add?"

"The Iroquois are better behaved than the Hurons," Andoura replied. "Tonneraont and Tsondacoué are fortunate to be attending this meeting. If the Seneca had not adopted them, they would still be wandering around like stray dogs. Just remember, Tonneraont: it was the Iroquois who vanquished the Hurons, not the French. You are no match for us."

The Seneca chief accompanying the Hurons began to speak.

"Tonneraont and Tsondacoué are two of the hundreds of Hurons who fought the French before they lost their country. If there had been more of them, perhaps they would have been able to save it. We are glad the Hurons were able to become good Iroquois. They are our brothers now. It would be wise to heed their warning."

"Your Huron brothers hate the French more than anyone," Andoura replied drily. "I agree their naïveté should be a lesson to us all. Let us squeeze more out of the French without allowing ourselves to be led by them—as they led the Hurons, who only have themselves to blame."

Ononta the shaman interrupted angrily.

"We should never have let the Blackrobes build a chapel in Onondaga! Awenissera has made a grave mistake in letting them settle among us. We should have stood our ground,

THE OTHER SIDE OF THE COIN

despite their threats. Now that their Great Spirit is among us, the danger is greater than ever."

Takanissorens tried to restore order.

"Everyone will have a chance to speak. Please, wait your turn. Tsondacoué, tell us how things went in your country."

The second Huron was calmer than the first. He spoke in a serious voice, looking at each of the chiefs in turn.

"We have always been a great nation," he began. "For generations, we have reached out to our partners. Our presence has been welcomed to the east, west, north, and south of our country. Our words have found an audience everywhere. When the Frenchmen arrived, we became allies because we have always been keen to trade and because they had so many goods to offer us, goods we did not know and that were precious to us. As the Iroquois know, this alliance bore fruit. In the beginning, it helped us find new partners and expand our influence. We were stronger. Then the Blackrobes settled among us. As soon as they arrived, they wanted to change our customs. They had a way with words; they were powerful and convincing. Many listened to them. They renounced our ancestors and learned to worship their Great Spirit. That's when everything changed. Disease ravaged our people. Everywhere, chiefs, warriors, women, and children died in hundreds. Our shamans were powerless to keep the evil at bay. The French would not listen to us. They did as they pleased. Then the Iroquois struck. They wiped out our nation when it was but a shadow of itself. Now the Hurons have been scattered to the four winds. That's what the Blackrobes have brought us…"

Tsondacoué had finished speaking. A heavy silence fell on the assembly. Seen in this light, the drama the Hurons had been through seemed inconceivable. And yet everyone knew that Tsondacoué was telling the truth. They also knew that such drama could happen again. The French posed a terrible threat.

Ononta broke the silence.

"Disease has already struck us down, and our spirits are powerless to cure us. We need to send the Frenchmen on their way while there is still time."

"The Dutch, too, brought disease to the Mohawks," Andoura retorted. "And yet you don't hear our brothers complaining. Far from it. The Great Spirit of the white men wishes us no harm; it can also be helpful and kind. Look at yourselves. You're all wearing a blanket that the French or Dutch exchanged for your furs. The Mohawks scoff at us with their Dutch muskets. How many victories have iron weapons brought us? How much effort have iron tools spared us? The Great Spirit of the white men is also working *for* us, my brothers. Let us not turn our backs on the French because the Hurons let themselves be taken in. Let us be wiser than they and restrict the French influence without forcing them to leave."

"Nonsense!" exclaimed the Mohawk chief who had been urging the Onondaga to break the peace for weeks. "Andoura is confusing everything. Our fathers imposed their will on the Dutch with their arms. Now the Dutch stay home in their villages and do what the Mohawks tell them. You must do the same with the French. You must vanquish them and show them who's in charge. The Mohawks will show you the path to follow. Do as we do. The Onondaga behave like women. They allow themselves to be led about by the nose and their attitude leaves us open to great misfortune. If the Onondaga are afraid of the French, let them call on the Mohawks, who will show them the path to victory. Because a Mohawk fears nothing. He is the most powerful of all."

Takanissorens grimaced as he glanced at the Cayuga and Seneca chiefs who had not yet spoken. They could no longer bear the Mohawks' arrogance and had met the previous day to agree on the message they wanted to convey. The other chiefs gave a slight nod to show that Takanissorens could express their point of view.

"It is not the first time we have heard this story from Osweati," Takanissorens began firmly. "We have heard it from the mouths of plenty of Mohawk chiefs who consider themselves to be masters of the Iroquois Confederacy. We have had enough. The Mohawks are too vain to realize that they are the ones threatening the League of Five Nations through their pride and injustices. Are you speaking on your nation's behalf, Osweati? Who gave you the mandate to spout such nonsense? Give me the names of the chiefs who insult us through your words."

Osweati tried to reply, but Takanissorens cut him off.

"Be quiet. Listen to what we have to tell you. Because I am speaking on behalf of the war chiefs from the other four nations of the Confederacy. This is what you can tell your Mohawk brothers."

Takanissorens—the bravest and most successful Onondaga war chief—was not going to be talked down to by anyone, especially not in Onondaga, which had always been the centre of the Iroquois Confederacy.

"The Mohawks are not wise enough to understand why we welcomed the French among us. Or perhaps they're pretending not to understand. Know that all of us—Onondaga, Seneca, Cayuga, and Oneida—invited the French because our Mohawk brothers have been turning a deaf ear to our pleas for years. Less than a moon ago, the Frenchmen gave us more powder than the Mohawks ever have. The French repair our muskets, while the Mohawks couldn't care less. The French give us more furs than the Mohawks who claim to be our brothers but keep everything for themselves. Osweati is threatening our

Confederacy with great misfortune if the Frenchmen stay among us. He is mistaken. For too long now, the Mohawks have been trying to dominate us, in spite of our traditions. For too long now, the Mohawks have been looking down on our brothers and looking to reduce them to slaves. You, Osweati, you are even arrogant enough to demand that we send the French on their way under the command of the Mohawks, while the French give us everything we need to destroy the Mohawks. Listen very carefully. While we continue to discuss matters of concern to us, you are going to return to your nation and tell all your war chiefs, all your peace chiefs, and all your clan mothers that if our Mohawk brothers do not undertake to give us equal access to the Dutch goods, if they do not agree to regain the place that is theirs within our Confederacy— keepers of the eastern door, and not the centre door or the door at the top—well then the Mohawks can prepare for war. Contrary to what you believe, we do not fear the Mohawks or the French or the Dutch. If your nation does not mend its ways, we will destroy it like we destroyed the Hurons. The League's other four nations will at last have access to all the goods they desire from the Dutch, or the French, whichever they prefer. I am giving the Mohawks one moon to reply. If not, then war it is. Now go. We have much to work out among ourselves."

Despite everyone's delight in spending Christmas together at the French fort, the information the missionaries and Radisson had come back with had been a blow. Each missionary had identified in his village one or more chiefs who were openly hostile to the French. Baptisms in particular were met with more and more fear and disapproval since they were viewed as a means of casting a spell on the Iroquois.

Radisson had witnessed more and more diplomatic visits in Onondaga. An impressive delegation of Mohawks, which included two war chiefs from his old village, had come bearing wampums. An impressive ceremony had been held at the Confederacy council house. Delegations from other nations had followed days later.

According to Radisson's sources, things had taken a dramatic turn for the French. By their calculations, a majority of chiefs were now against the alliance. A rumour was even circulating in the village that the French were being fattened like pigs for slaughter. The Iroquois intended to keep them in the fort all winter, like pigs in a pen, before executing them in the spring.

The Iroquois were convinced that the men they now looked upon as their prisoners were incapable of returning to New France by their own means. They were at their mercy; and the Iroquois were in no great hurry. They also believed they had no inkling of the fate that awaited them. As they waited to exterminate the French who had come to live in their country, the Iroquois wanted to make the most of the gunsmith and the blacksmith, who repaired their muskets and made the iron items they needed, for as long as possible. They continued to trade with the French, vowing that they would take back all the furs they exchanged.

The situation was so serious that Superior Le Mercier believed the time had come to inform Commander Dupuys, although he was sworn to secrecy. It was vital that the Frenchmen in the fort not panic or act rashly and aggravate matters.

"Our priority," Father Ragueneau explained to Commander Dupuys, "is to save every last Frenchman. One false move and many will die. That's a certainty. And it is to be avoided at all costs."

Dismayed at a threat he hadn't seen coming, Zacharie Dupuys was lost for words.

"We must return to our communities," said Ragueneau. "Otherwise the Iroquois will see that we know what they're up to and might attack right away. We need to play for time."

"We need a plan," added Father Le Moyne. "For as long as we don't have a detailed plan to get ourselves out of this mess, there's no point letting anyone know. There are already eight of us in the know. That's plenty."

Radisson, who had been looking for a way out for days, began to speak.

"We need a ploy to outwit the Iroquois. I know them well enough to know that it's best to outsmart them rather than confront them. I have an idea..."

|||||||||||||||||||||||||||||||||||||||||||||||||||||||||||||||||||||||||||||||||||||||||||||||||||

CHAPTER 5

SAVING THE FRENCH

THE FOUR MEN TRUDGED FORWARD, heads down against the flurry of snow. Huge snowflakes smacked against their faces. The weather was unrecognizable from the sunshine that had marked their departure from the fort. Violent, snowy gusts blocked the sun a second time and caught them by surprise on the path to Onondaga.

It was a day of surprises.

Radisson was pulling one of two sleds laden with goods to be traded. Vincent Prudhomme and Father Ragueneau walked ahead. Their snowshoes flattened the terrain, making it easier for the sleds to follow behind. Robert Racine brought up the rear. Commander Dupuys had imposed new rules since Christmas: there was to be no travelling in groups of less than three. The official reason was to make sure no goods were stolen and to keep everyone safe in the wintry conditions. Ragueneau was returning to his post as a missionary. His three companions would travel back and forth between the fort and the village to step up trade.

Radisson was struck by the magic of winter. The tangled silhouettes of bare tree trunks, half white with snow, stretched as far as the eye could see. They were interspersed with towering balsam firs, crowned with white branches, ghostly intruders in this deciduous forest. When everything was swallowed up for an instant in the squall, it seemed like a fairy wand was busily painting the forest white.

Once they reached the village, the four Frenchmen headed straight to the home behind the chapel, where Ragueneau and visiting Frenchmen stayed. It was also used to store trading goods because the Iroquois believed the Jesuits were protecting the house with magical powers. They were safe there. Only Radisson was to stay in the Turtle clan longhouse with Andoura. Ragueneau had consented, although hesitantly. Once the home for the Frenchmen had been heated and the trading goods were unwrapped, Radisson got ready to leave. He chose and hastily bundled together items for Andoura's family.

"Are you certain it's a good idea?" Ragueneau asked him again, out of earshot of Prudhomme and Racine.

"I already told you, Father," Radisson whispered back. "The longer I spend with the Iroquois, the more they trust me. That's how I get my best information."

The Jesuit noticed the eagle feather attached to a leather lace that Radisson had tied around his neck.

"Now what is that? Isn't that taking things a little too far? Just be careful you don't turn back into an Iroquois."

Radisson didn't want to reveal the real reason for his attachment to the feather and the others he had left behind at the fort. Ragueneau would be annoyed and would no doubt hold it against him.

"Andoura's daughter gave it to me," he claimed. "Her family will be pleased to see me wearing it."

"A woman now!" Ragueneau exclaimed, doing his best to keep his voice down. "That's all we need! Just be careful, Radisson. Love can turn a man's head. Remember that the fate of the French lies largely in your hands. If ever you were to tell her too much..."

"Don't worry, Father. I know what I'm doing. My plan is a good one, and I'm not enough of an idiot to ruin everything for the sake of a pretty smile."

"The Indian women have much more to offer than just a pretty smile, my poor child..."

"Andoura is waiting for me. I have to go. I'll be in touch soon, Father."

Andoura welcomed Radisson with open arms. Lavionkié came over to join them right away.

"What did you bring?" she asked Radisson, staring at him with her big, bright eyes.

"Take a look," he said, unpacking the goods.

Radisson was won over by the happiness radiating from the young woman. He forgot Andoura for a moment. She seemed even more beautiful than in the dreams he had at the fort. Turning each object carefully in her hands, she stopped to give him a red-hot look. Radisson couldn't take his eyes off her graceful body, her hair glistening in the light of the fire, her angelic face.

Andoura could see the two were both hopelessly in love. The thought had crossed his mind, but now it was clear for all to see. Ogienda, who had known for a while now, was less enthusiastic than her husband about the relationship. Andoura could see no objection: his daughter was happy, Radisson too, and having a French trader in the family would no doubt come in handy. Ogienda worried that people in the village were claiming to be allies of the French through thick and thin, while others were already turning their backs on them.

Lavionkié sat down to take in all the goods she had scattered on the ground. She had never seen so much—all shiny new—within reach. Her eyes gleamed. Radisson was elated. He felt as though the world was only just beginning. Lavionkié took a blanket, squeezed it between her delicate fingers, and brought it to her cheek. The red cloth accentuated her dark skin.

"It's so soft," she said, ecstatic.

Radisson couldn't resist.

"You can keep it."

Lavionkié was set aglow in a blaze of happiness, like a forest set ablaze by a gust of wind. Her eyes were limpid. Radisson dove in, as into an ocean. The distance between Onondaga and Trois-Rivières was behind them. Nothing else could ever come between them. As lithe as a cat, Lavionkié stood to kiss him. The Frenchman's head was spinning. In his culture, such outward displays of affection weren't permitted before marriage. But they were here. Lavionkié's body became one with his, openly, boldly. Radisson could barely breathe.

The rest of the evening was spent around the fire. Lavionkié didn't let go of her sweetheart, caressing him with her hand, shoulder, or leg. The Frenchman gradually grew used to her touch and regained some of his composure. Ogienda gave them something to eat, silently remaining in the background. One of the couple's sons ate with them, but Radisson barely noticed. Late that evening, he gave a knife blade to Andoura and a copper pot to Ogienda. He then put away his goods underneath the bed that had been set aside for him. As he tried to fall asleep, he was surprised at just how at ease he felt here, despite the fate that lay in store for the French. This house was a haven of peace.

The following day, Radisson waited until Ogienda had put her daughter to work before he got up. From his bed, he couldn't help but admire the grace and determination Lavionkié put into crushing corn in a huge wooden mortar.

But there was something he needed to do and he couldn't allow himself to be distracted. Once he was out of bed, he walked Andoura over to an empty corner of the house to let him know of some of the decisions made by the French.

"We are courageous. We do not fear death," Radisson told him. "That's why we will do everything we can to convince the Iroquois that the French are their best allies. We want to prove that it is better for you to trade with us than with the Dutch. We want to join forces with the Iroquois forever, and we are prepared to do anything to see that happen. You will not be disappointed you supported us, Andoura. You will see we can be of use to you, even more useful than you think. But if we are to succeed, we need the support of all those who are still our friends. I need you, Andoura."

Radisson paused to see what impact his words were having, and to make sure the chief had not changed camp while he had been away. Andoura took a few moments to take everything in. Since the Mohawks had responded favourably to the other Iroquois nations, he believed the alliance with the French to be lost forever. He had given up siding with the French in public, even though his feelings had not changed. But Radisson's words rekindled his hope. Perhaps it might still be possible to avoid war. Perhaps the alliance and peace could be saved. It was his duty to at least try, to make one last effort.

"Your words hearten me greatly," he replied. "You are right. Perhaps we can reconcile our peoples. How can I help you?"

Radisson had scored a point. At the very least, he had to keep this influential ally on their side; Andoura was one of the few that remained. But he was aiming higher than that.

"I promise you," Radisson went on, "there will be fewer baptisms. We want to reassure our brothers who are worried, and convince them that our Great Spirit is the most powerful, that he can help you. At the next full moon, we will celebrate an important festival in our religion: Candlemas. We want to celebrate with you. We will invite all the Iroquois to a huge feast we will be giving that day. Out of love for our Iroquois brothers and love for our Great Spirit. I ask you to please convince the people of Onondaga to come in droves, especially those who wish to wage war against us again. It is they who should understand that the Frenchmen are great and that it is best to keep the peace with them. Can you help me, Andoura?"

"Readily," he replied. "You can count on me."

Father Le Moyne had been right. Ouatsouan was easily bribed and had been a surprisingly reliable informant. Even though Radisson could no longer stand the sight of him, he had to visit him once more.

Ouatsouan greeted him with his usual two-faced smile. As usual, they sat around the fire of his family of origin, in the Deer clan house. Ouatsouan had married a woman from the Turtle clan, but his wife had left him after a year or two. He had had to return to his mother's house, where he now lived as a bachelor.

Ouatsouan gave Radisson something to eat, making a show of revering the young Frenchman who deigned to trade with such a humble man, even though he wasn't a chief like his brother Awenissera, a shaman, or a famous warrior. This was part of the smoke and mirrors surrounding their secret agreement. His attitude grated on Radisson's nerves as Ouatsouan milked his role for all he was worth. He might have been worth his weight in gold to the French as they made the most of his greed, but Radisson couldn't understand why his information was always so specific each time he betrayed his brothers. A love of personal possessions had led to a slippery slope. To cover himself, Ouatsouan made sure everyone thought he was fond of stealing French goods.

The scrawny Iroquois with the devilish eyes handed him a beaver pelt and a deer hide. Radisson felt them between his fingers to gauge their worth.

"I'm feeling generous today. I'll give you three axes and five knives. It's a very good price."

"That's all?" Ouatsouan replied. "That's not much for such fine pelts."

"I don't need the deer. Give me another beaver pelt and you can have what you want."

"But the deer hide is so soft... I'm sure Lavionkié would love it."

How did he do it? How did this man manage to find out so much? Radisson had never been seen in public with Lavionkié. Someone must have been spying on him and talking behind his back. He would have to be more careful.

"Very well," said Radisson, keen to bring the deal to a close. "I can give you five axes and five knives. That's all I have with me. It's a very good deal for you."

"I know. You are good to me. You make me so happy."

And now he was making fun of him...

"If you have other pelts for me," added Radisson, as he laid out the axe and knife blades at the Iroquois' feet, "let me know and I'll come back. You know where to find me."

"In Lavionkié's arms or at my dear brother Awenissera's house, yes, yes, I know."

"Go to hell," Radisson thought.

He stood and motioned for Ouatsouan to follow him. They walked over to one of the doors of the house, where nobody could hear them, and Radisson added softly:

"I left a barrel of powder in the usual place. Be quick about it. It's going to be dark tonight. Make the most of it."

It was Ouatsouan's turn to look around.

"After the last big hunts," he whispered, "in the springtime, the younger warriors are going to come for you..."

He sliced his hand across his throat with a grin.

"Thank you," said Radisson, eager to leave now.

After the big hunts... That didn't leave much time to put their plan into action.

Vincent and Robert were preparing the sleds outside Ragueneau's cabin. They were getting ready to return to the fort with Radisson to leave the pelts there and bring back new goods to trade. Radisson made the most of his time alone with the Jesuit, inside the house.

"We need more canoes," he said.

"We can't very well ask the Iroquois for them," Ragueneau replied. "It's the middle of winter. They'll be suspicious."

"Even in the spring, they'll say no. They're too clever to give us just what we need to slip away from them. We need another solution."

"Do you know how to make a birch-bark canoe? Do you know a Frenchman who can?"

"No. I've seen them do it, but I wouldn't be able to do it alone. You need to know what you're doing to make a canoe that's watertight and solid. The river will be rough. We'll need canoes that can stand up to anything."

"And the clock is ticking."

Both men thought hard.

"Perhaps I have an idea," said Radisson. "I'll ask the carpenter if he can put together some kind of flat-bottomed barge. If we tell him it's for moving the pelts, he won't suspect a thing."

"Good idea. Have a word with him as soon as you reach the fort. Things can't go on like this," the Jesuit added, once he had made sure they were still alone. "Soon we will have to let everyone know that our lives are in danger. We can't keep the truth from them any longer. Maybe fifty heads will come up with better solutions."

"If you think that's necessary, Father. But I would wait, if I were you. According to what I'm hearing, lots of Iroquois will be coming to the feast. If all goes according to plan, we'll have better news to give them after Candlemas."

"Very well. Let's give your plan a chance first. Speaking of which, I want you to stay at the fort until I arrive with the Iroquois. Send someone else back here with Vincent and Robert. I have a few things I want you to prepare to help your plan along."

"At your service, Father."

Before leaving the village, Radisson passed by to say hello to Andoura and make sure he was bringing as many people as possible to the party. He knew that Lavionkié and Ogienda would not be coming. Andoura was already close enough to the French as it was. There was no need to fan the flames.

They walked out of their way to avoid passing in front of the Bear clan house. Even though Radisson would have liked to visit Mahatari and Ononta, he feared the shaman might discover his secret. He had started avoiding their house and took care not to bump into them in the village.

At the head of the procession making its way to the fort, Father Ragueneau held up a wooden cross as he chanted in praycr. The Jesuit had placed the procession under the protection of the Great Spirit of the French. The fifty or so Iroquois who followed one behind the other seemed impressed by the ritual, if a little suspicious. The feast would comfort them.

The gate to the fort opened wide to welcome them. Commander Dupuys, dressed in his finest clothes and wearing high leather boots, with a sword in his belt and a feathered hat on his head, kept to the centre of the group. Two Jesuits and several other Frenchmen surrounded him to form a guard of honour. Radisson was pleased to see so many Iroquois had turned out, given how few allies they still had left in Onondaga. As Ragueneau had asked, he was posted by the entrance, handing out small candles.

"You will light them shortly to seek the favour of our Great Spirit. Come in. The celebrations are just getting started."

He had done the same thing the night before, when two small groups of Iroquois had arrived from the two villages where Father Ménard and Father Dablon lived permanently. Father Frémin and Father Le Mercier had been deemed to live too far away to take part in the celebrations.

Outside the fort, the French had built a large shelter in which to serve the meal that would last all night. First, a welcoming ceremony was held inside the perimeter. All the Iroquois were now gathered by the two large fires that had just been lit. In the pale twilight, Commander Dupuys got the celebrations underway by thanking the Iroquois for coming in such numbers. He urged them to enjoy the gargantuan meal the French had prepared for their friends for Candlemas, as was their custom. Then he invited Father Le Moyne to speak.

"You know me," said the Jesuit. "You welcomed me as a brother many moons ago, and for that I will be eternally grateful to you. Since then, several Frenchmen have joined me in this country that we love, a country where we share your sorrows and your joys as one people. And that is why we are so happy to celebrate with you one of our religion's biggest festivals: Candlemas. It symbolizes the divine light, the strength of the sun and the hope for better days ahead. In a moment, we will be serving up a feast that you won't soon forget. But first, allow me to introduce Father Ragueneau, whom some of you already know. Others have never met him since he arrived here only a short time ago. Father Ragueneau was keen to share this moment with you to show how delighted he is to be living among you."

Radisson's job was to watch the Iroquois' reaction at this point. While Ragueneau took Le Moyne's place on the little platform, Radisson saw that they were all a little taken aback by so much kindness. Even those he knew to be ferocious enemies of the French appeared flattered. Ragueneau continued the charm offensive.

"My brothers," he said, in a loud, booming voice. "Thank you for responding in such numbers to our invitation. Nowhere can the French count on such a precious ally as the Iroquois. I have discovered them to be a great people and today I am delighted to share with you the goodness of our God, the one you call the Great Spirit. May he bestow upon you as much power and advantage as he has given the French for generations.

"The feast of Candlemas is one of our finest festivals: it marks the return of the light. It celebrates the glory of our God who reigns in heaven, like the sun that warms our hearts. At Candlemas, we traditionally serve round cakes to remind us of the sun you worship. These we call pancakes. We made them with the corn flour you so generously gave us. They are yellow like the sun, a symbol of our unbreakable, life-giving union.

"But this is only a beginning. We will soon be serving all the food you love so much: roasted meat, bear fat, and smoked fish. Because we very much want to thank you for bringing peace to our peoples. Thank you, my Iroquois brothers. Thank you from the bottom of my heart. Now, let us light our candles to give thanks to the generosity of our God. We will now move to where the feast will be served. Let us go eat, my brothers! And may God bless us!"

While the French lit the candles with small torches, the Jesuits took their place at the head of the procession, holding their crosses high for all to see. They walked to the shelter that had been put up against the palisade. There the ground was covered with balsam boughs and beaver pelts so that the Iroquois could sit in comfort. Three large fires had been lit before the shelter, each the same distance apart, so that the smoke would not bother the guests as the fires kept them warm. A handful of people immediately served pancakes on wooden plates.

"Eat until you can eat no more!" Ragueneau cried. "There's plenty for everyone, as much as you like! Celebrate the light of the world, our Jesus, our God! Enjoy your meal, my brothers!"

The food kept on coming all night long. Heavy pots filled to the brim with meat, fish, sagamité, and fat were brought out from the kitchens. The Iroquois were both surprised and delighted. From time to time, a Jesuit would say a prayer, sing a psalm, or hold a brief sermon on the glory and power of God. Radisson checked in occasionally to make sure the guests were stuffing themselves. The Frenchmen inside the fort were given the same treatment, having been forewarned that the feast was essential to staying on good terms with the Iroquois. They had no reason to be jealous.

Everything went as planned.

By the early hours of the morning, not a single Iroquois could eat another bite. They had eaten their fill. Father Ragueneau spoke to them.

"You can see just how much the French love the Iroquois. There will be more feasts like this one to celebrate our Great Spirit, other celebrations you will be invited to. But the time has come to go back to your villages. Father Ménard, Father Dablon, and I will go with you. As a token of our friendship and to show you that we respect your customs as much as you respect our own, we ask that you place the homeward journey under the protection of the spirits of your ancestors. Now relax a moment longer. Take your time. Whenever you are ready, we will trust in your chiefs and your spirits. Whenever you are ready, my brothers."

His legs weary from overeating, but his chest swollen with pride, the old chief Awenissera headed the procession back to the villages. His satisfaction was immense. Now it would be easier to silence those who had been more and more openly criticizing the alliance with the French. Even Takanissorens was questioning himself as he walked behind Awenissera. At last, the Jesuits were honouring their spirits. But were flattery and a good meal reason enough to forget the grave dangers the French posed to their country? Much was at stake. All things considered, there was something suspect about this abrupt change of mind. Better to continue to fight the alliance with the French. Although now the threat seemed less pressing; the advantages of them being there seemed to weigh more in the balance. He no longer felt compelled to act so urgently.

Andoura walked ahead of Radisson and Father Ragueneau, in the group of leaders. His young friend had been telling the truth. The French were skilful and were doing everything in their power to win back the hearts of the Iroquois. But he feared it would not be enough to get those who wanted to kill or capture the French to ignore the threat of death hanging over them. Many of the more skeptical Iroquois had been absent as well. The battle was far from won.

Most of the Iroquois in the procession had been too exhausted by the night of feasting to ponder the question. They were glad to have eaten so well and were in a rush to return home to rest. There would be time later to reconsider the pros and cons of the alliance.

The trail that led to the village was not difficult. Even in winter, it was almost as hard and flat as a trail in summer, thanks to the comings and goings of the fur trade. Which didn't stop Father Ragueneau getting his feet caught up in his snowshoes and falling headfirst into the snow. Fortunately, he came to no harm.

"Careful!" Andoura and Radisson chorused as they helped him up.

The chiefs at the head of the group stopped for a moment to inquire after the missionary. They offered to slacken the pace, but Ragueneau replied it was nothing but a moment of clumsiness and they could continue as before.

They reached the only hilly part of the journey, where the trail edged its way along a hillside overlooking the river. Only one person could pass at a time, taking care not to slip. It was here that Ragueneau fell a second time, tumbling down the rocky slope and down onto the frozen shoreline. Once he had stopped rolling, the Jesuit let out a harrowing cry. He appeared to be seriously hurt.

Ten Iroquois removed their snowshoes and carefully made their way down to him. When they tried to help him to his feet and back up the slope, the Jesuit's cries grew louder. Radisson asked the Iroquois to leave him where he was.

"What's wrong, Father?" he asked. "Where does it hurt?"

SAVING THE FRENCH

"Everywhere!" Ragueneau responded, his voice choked with emotion. "Ouch! Don't touch me!"

Awenissera and Takanissorens were concerned at the reaction of a missionary who had proven his endurance many times before. It was a terrible stroke of misfortune; no one had ever injured themselves on this stretch of trail before. Takanissorens scrambled down to see him. He gently probed at his body. Ragueneau let out a roar when he touched his right leg. Takanissorens immediately sent for a branch and a piece of cloth to hold the Jesuit's leg in place. Despite the priest's litany of complaints, he worked skilfully, and within seconds Ragueneau was back on his feet again. Ragueneau gritted his teeth as he moaned and groaned. He appeared close to fainting.

Once he was safely back up on the trail, the missionary seemed in such pain that he no longer made a sound. His face was white. Radisson had never seen him in such a state.

"We need to bring him back to the fort and quickly," said Radisson. "Our surgeon will take care of him. We'll have to carry him. He can no longer walk."

Takanissorens was dismayed that the calamity had struck when they had been under the protection of the Iroquois spirits. He was eager to hear what the French surgeon had to say about the injury. Almost all the Iroquois continued on to Onondaga. Takanissorens, Andoura, Radisson, and another Iroquois he did not know carried the Jesuit back to the fort.

When they arrived, the surgeon felt Father Ragueneau's leg and the priest screamed in pain. The surgeon, a man well used to suffering, fought back tears at the sight of the man of the cloth in such agony.

"We'll have to put your leg in plaster right away, Father. Your leg is broken in two places. You'll feel better after that, I promise. It's just a bad patch you'll have to get through. You'll get better. I can assure you of that."

Radisson translated his diagnosis for the Iroquois chiefs. It was painful, but nothing too serious. Ragueneau's life was not in any danger. The Iroquois were partly reassured, but disappointed that the French celebrations had ended so badly for the man who had organized them.

"I'll come back and visit him," said Takanissorens. "We will ask our spirits to watch over him and heal him."

The three Iroquois left right away to make sure the night did not surprise them on their way home. Radisson stayed by his master's bedside to help him through this difficult time. Father Le Moyne also came to offer his friend his support while the surgeon went about making the plaster. Ragueneau managed to keep his pain under control. He remained stoical, then fell asleep with exhaustion, lying motionless in the bed the surgeon had made up for him next to his.

The time had now come to warn all the French about the change in the Iroquois' intentions. Since Father Ragueneau could not do it himself, the delicate undertaking fell to Commander Dupuys, Father Le Moyne, and Radisson. They had all agreed to express their hope that the peace might hold. But Radisson was under no illusions. He believed the plan should be applied in full until they returned to Montréal.

The men gathered in the Jesuit accommodations, a place they normally did not enter. They suspected something was amiss, no doubt something to do with Father Ragueneau injuring himself the night before. The tiny room was full to capacity. Commander Dupuys and Father Le Moyne stood next to the stone fireplace, where a huge fire had been lit. Radisson sat next to them.

"My friends," the commander declared. "We have learned that a number of Iroquois are working to undermine our alliance with them. Some of them want to see our ruin. We organized the feast in the hopes of thwarting them. But we do not know how the situation will evolve from here. We are in danger."

A deathly silence fell over the stunned assembly.

"But fear not: we have an escape plan if things get any worse."

"For several months now," Father Le Moyne cut in, seeing faces harden, "Mohawk chiefs have been trying to persuade the Onondaga to go back to war with us. But they have not yet succeeded. The chiefs who remain loyal to us are keeping us informed of their every move. We hope that—"

The Jesuit didn't get a chance to finish his sentence. The room erupted.

"We'll kill them!" René Dufresne cried. "I told you we couldn't trust those Iroquois dogs!"

"We'll kill them before they kill us!" another cried.

"The feast was a huge success," Dupuys interjected. "We can still turn this around..."

The room was again in an uproar. Men were beating the tables with their fists, cursing like sailors. Father Le Moyne intervened, waving his arms in the air.

"My brothers! My brothers! Calm down! We are not at risk. As the commander told you, we have a plan and we are going to get ourselves out of this mess, whatever happens. Now listen up!"

A murmur washed across the room like a wave, interrupted only by the occasional growl and exclamation.

"Listen to us!" Father Le Moyne repeated. "We're going to need each and every one of you if we are to come out of this with our lives. Listen to your commander!"

Silence was gradually restored, although it was unsteady and fragile.

"We know that the Iroquois will not attempt anything before spring, even if those in favour of war gain the upper hand!" shouted Zacharie Dupuys. "They think there's no way we can escape from their clutches, but that's where they're wrong! We'll all go back to the colony if need be, every last one of us. We'll use our canoes and the flat-bottomed boats we've started building. We'll be ready in time. They won't be able to lay a finger on us. Just listen to our plan..."

"We'll attack their villages!" Dufresne cried again. "Death to the traitors!"

"We'll kill them all! Let's attack!"

Radisson climbed up onto his chair to interrupt.

"The Iroquois will follow you to the gates of hell if you attack their villages! They will kill your children and your children's children! Their vengeance will be without end! I know them. I lived among them. Behind every Iroquois that you kill, ten, then one hundred more will stand up and take his place, until the French have been wiped off the map. Only ignorance and anger can make you think that fifty Frenchmen stand a chance against five hundred Iroquois warriors. If you want to save your lives, listen to what we have prepared. Cunning will save us, not brute force."

Radisson could see the anger some of the men had for the Jesuits. They had walked them into this trap after turning a deaf ear to the men of experience who had warned them not to come. He could see them shooting daggers at Father Le Moyne. But that didn't change the situation. Anger was a bad counsellor. Commander Dupuys tried to regain control.

"We need you! I am your commander, and you are going to do what I tell you! If we stick together, it's a foregone conclusion. We'll return to the colony safe and sound, if we have to go that far. Rebels be warned: I'll put you in irons if I have to. Saving us all depends on everyone following orders. One false step from one man among us could lead to the downfall of us all. The Iroquois have no idea we know what they're up to. We start with an advantage over them. Allies are still defending our cause. So be quiet and listen to what we have to say. Our plan is working. It's already underway."

Reason at last won out over anger. Radisson got back down off his chair. There was no need to say anything else for the moment.

CHAPTER 6

FLIGHT

R ADISSON SPENT DAYS going around villages with Prudhomme and Racine to meet all the missionaries and find out the latest news. Several sources confirmed that the Iroquois had decided at a grand council of the nation to rid themselves of the French once the big winter hunts were over. There was no hope of a change of heart. A majority of chiefs and clan mothers now openly showed their opposition to the Jesuits, who epitomized all they feared about the French. Officially, Radisson and his companions were there to trade. And trade was brisk. Things would have looked very different had they only been there to exchange goods. But it was their religion, too, their fort, their intrusive ways, and the illnesses the French brought with them that spread panic and had led to the Iroquois rejecting them.

As soon as the Iroquois left the villages for their hunting ground, trade ground to a halt. While there was still time, Radisson took the opportunity to return to Onondaga to spend a few days with the Iroquois who were dear to him: Lavionkié and Andoura.

The Turtle clan house was busy, despite the hunters' absence. A handful of Iroquois were gathered two fires down from Andoura's. They were having a great time playing knuckle-bones, and now and then one of them would suddenly burst out laughing. Radisson tried to ignore the distraction.

The previous day, messengers had come to announce that Father Ragueneau was better. It was the sign they had agreed on to launch the plan's final phase. Radisson, who was still eager to find out just how Andoura had gotten his eagle-head knife, had realized that they had never spoken of it. At his request, Andoura got ready to tell him a story he had told many times before. Ogienda and Lavionkié, who well knew this episode of his life, stayed by his side all the same, close by the fire in a respectful silence.

"I was a young man," began Andoura, "a little younger than you. It was my first war expedition. I wanted to prove my courage and bring back many scalps. Our chief, who is now dead—taken by the illnesses of the white men—was a man of experience. He had gone to war several times with the nations of the west and won many victories. Shortly before we left, he had a dream he spoke of often during the expedition."

Sitting on the ground with his legs crossed, Andoura stared straight ahead, lost in thought, as he recalled these distant events. Radisson was hanging on his every word, hoping to shed some light on the mystery surrounding their knives.

"Our chief had dreamt that beyond all the territories where he had been, he would find a country that was richer, more abundant in game, more fertile, and almost as beautiful as the land where our ancestors lie. He was determined to make it there, and convinced us to follow him right to the end. We paddled and hiked for days and days. Whenever we met our enemies, he ordered us to hide. We clashed with no one. Further on, he said, we would find greater spoils and better opportunities to distinguish ourselves in combat. Our nation would be proud of the land we were to discover."

This wonderful mirage still shone brightly in Andoura's eyes. Radisson thought back to his expedition in the land of the Erie.

"The further we advanced into unknown territory, the more excited our chief grew. We were only seven. The danger was great. I was the youngest and I was afraid, but I followed my chief without complaint. I wanted to become a man. One night, while we slept, a great number of warriors took us by surprise and captured us. They brought us to the large village where they lived. We did not know their language, but a prisoner who had become their slave spoke our language well. The man was not mistreated. They had cut off two fingers from each hand so that he could no longer fight. He served a shaman and perhaps himself knew the language of the spirits. He was a good man."

Andoura broke off to take a sip of water and calm the emotions that were still raging twenty-five years later. Radisson was impressed, as always, by the daring of the Iroquois warriors.

"That man saved our lives," Andoura went on. "He spoke with his heart when he translated my words to justify our being in the land of the nation that had made us prisoners. We had killed no one. We had no scalps with us, no spoils. I spoke to him of Deganawidah. I told him we had ventured so far because our chief had a vision. He wanted to propose peace with the great people we were going to meet so that the Iroquois would form a strong, united nation with this people. The interpreter believed me and translated my words with conviction. From an apprentice warrior who had not yet killed or wounded a single person, that day I became a voice for peace. My lie saved us, because the village chief accepted the alliance I was proposing. He promised to send us back safe and sound to our country to announce the news to our people. From that day forward, our two nations would be united forever. My words of peace had earned us a great victory. My future had been plotted. The spirits had been clear."

"And the knife?" asked Radisson. "You haven't mentioned the knife."

Andoura unsheathed his knife and rested it in the palms of his hands as he had done in Trois-Rivières. Radisson and he watched it carefully in the light of the fire.

"The village shaman made it. Before we left, he took the iron knife I was wearing. Nobody in the village had ever seen iron, aside from the interpreter. A few people had small bits of copper on them, which they had gotten from neighbouring nations they traded with. But they had never seen such big pieces of metal—so hard and sharp—as our iron knives and axes. They were very impressed. The shaman made the handle of my knife from the horns of an animal we saw over there. It was huge and very strong. It gave them all they needed. They called it a buffalo. He fashioned the handle into an eagle head because we had come from far away, from an unknown land, as though we had flown over lakes and forests. I swore I would take care of it as a sign of the alliance between both our peoples, an alliance that went beyond our differences, like an eagle soaring in the sky and coming back down to earth to feed."

Andoura looked up at Radisson and appeared stunned.

"I do not understand why your knife is identical to mine. It was made for me, and you never went there. I do not understand..."

Radisson was just as mystified as he was.

"And yet it was the same person who made them. I don't see any other explanation."

Their eyes met. It was a fascinating story that confirmed all that Radisson had been through since leaving his Iroquois family. He was moving in the right direction, along the path of peace, like Andoura. But all was not yet clear.

The two women stood now that Andoura's story was over. Lavionkié tried to get Radisson's attention, and he was pulled from his thoughts, enchanted by her beauty. Lavionkié looked at him differently that evening. Her gaze was full of light, more intense. She wished him goodnight with a knowing look, then retired to her bed, in the half-dark at the side of the house. Radisson still felt as though she were beside him. Her shadow filled his heart. Ogienda went off to bed, too. Andoura and Radisson were alone.

A few fires down, the laughter from the group of Iroquois had died down. Only two or three of the men continued to chat around the dying embers of the fire.

"The chiefs met again," Andoura said, looking worried. "A grand council was held before the hunters left."

Radisson knew this already, but pretended not to. Their plan depended on his discretion.

"The efforts you made to honour us did not change the opinion of the majority of chiefs. The French are now in great danger. You must take care, when the hunters return. The Iroquois might attack you."

Radisson feigned surprise, delighted by Andoura's honesty. Then he puffed out his chest.

"No one will ever take our fort!" he replied, firmly but quietly so they would not be overheard. "The French fear nothing. If your warriors are foolish enough to attack us, then so be it! We will fight and defeat them. Too bad for them. But I am sure that your chiefs can still be convinced otherwise. We will host them for another important festival—Easter—which coincides with Father Ragueneau being back on his feet, I was told yesterday. The Iroquois will never have seen a celebration like it. I still want to fight for peace, Andoura, as you have done. Please do not abandon me. I ask that you stay strong. We can still do it."

Andoura answered with silence. He held out little hope of turning things around. Hardly any Iroquois now made a case for the French. Awenissera had been marginalized. The Mohawks and the Hurons had persuaded almost all the Onondaga to put an end to the French living among them. Now that the League of Five Nations had regained its cohesion, the disadvantages of allying with the French outweighed the advantages. It had been decided. Radisson shared this opinion, but he had to play his role right to the end.

"I promise you one thing," Andoura responded. "I will speak up for you. We will need an interpreter to negotiate with the French in the future. You know both languages well, and many Iroquois trust you more than any other Frenchman. Your life will be spared. I can promise you that. I will do for you what the interpreter I met so long ago did for me. I will not let you down."

"Thank you, Andoura. I am moved by your promise. But I do not want to think we will reach that point. The feast of Easter will be celebrated in style and we will implore our powerful God to come to our aid. Everyone will eat as much as they please, as is your tradition. The chiefs will have to come. Again I am counting on you to convince them to attend this great celebration."

"I admire your determination. I will help you, for it is my destiny. But keep in mind that the battle will be hard and per-haps in vain."

"Garagonké told me that it takes more courage to bring about peace than to win a war. I have this courage."

"So do I."

Andoura, too, went to bed for the night. Radisson remained alone, gazing at the flames that were born and died in the embers, flickering like the final steps of exhausted dancers. For all that, the embers were no less hot, and the trance was no less intense in the hearts of the shamans who had danced themselves to exhaustion. Radisson had no doubt that their plan was going to work now that Father Ragueneau had given the signal for the final stage. He was returning with valuable information from his stay with the Iroquois. He had not come in vain.

He had not heard the young woman come up to him, but suddenly he felt Lavionkié's warm hand on the back of his neck. He turned to speak to her, but she put a finger to her mouth right away to tell him to be quiet.

"Shh."

Lavionkié picked up a twig from the ground, set it alight in the embers, and held it up to Radisson's mouth. It meant "I want to make love to you." He blew on the flame by way of reply: "Me too." She led him by the hand to the area vacated by the neighbouring family, several members of which had gone hunting. Those left behind had temporarily moved in with another family. Lavionkié had it all planned out. She unfurled the bear and beaver pelts she had left on the ground and undressed. Then she helped Radisson take off his own clothes and remove the sheath for his knife. She pulled him to the ground beside her and covered him with another pelt. She kissed him passionately. Radisson grabbed at her, under the spell of his beautiful Iroquois.

From where he was, Radisson watched Ogienda get up first. She saw the couple lying in each other's arms beneath the pelts, but didn't take much notice. She had seen it coming for a while. It was too early to start worrying about the marriage their romance might lead to. Better to let them enjoy themselves in peace for the time being. Love could be fickle.

Radisson had woken up before everyone, as soon as the darkness had cleared. He intended to enjoy his last moments with Lavionkié, his wildflower, his sweetheart. He caressed her hips, her waist, her breasts, her face, her hair, her arms, her belly, her thighs, as soft as the silkiest fur, as warm as the most comforting hearth, as beautiful as the sun in the springtime. He would never tire of it. She was still half asleep, pressed tight against him, her back buried in his stomach, embedded in his flesh. She was a wonderful woman and he was free to marry her since they weren't from the same clan. But today he had to leave forever. It was better this way, even though it hurt. He didn't want to live his life among the Iroquois.

Andoura's offer hadn't changed his mind. There was no way he would allow himself to be a prisoner/interpreter. No way he would spend his days living in dread, afraid he would be executed because of a dream or because a chief was angry. He had already said no to this way of life. He would not be going back. He didn't want to bring Lavionkié with him either, far from her brothers and her country. She would be hated and despised by the French, just as he suffered here. Their love was a gift from heaven, wonderful but fleeting, like a ripe fruit that had to be enjoyed at just the right moment.

Radisson looked down at the eagle-head knife lying on the ground in front of him. For once, it wasn't pressed tight against his skin. He took stock and better understood the meaning he was to give it after Andoura had told him his story. Ononta did not know why the handle had been made. He did not know the powers the shaman from another country had invested in it. He had not been able to tell him everything.

Radisson could see more clearly now: his destiny would not stop here, nor in New France. He would have to go far out west to where the knife had been made, to where the knife was pulling him. It was showing him a direction to follow. His life was one of travel, discovery, and peace. His flight would have to take him further.

When he closed his eyes, Radisson felt as though he were slowly taking off, like an eagle spreading its wings. He felt completely free, ready to leave. The Iroquois were turning a deaf ear to the invitation extended to them by the French, but other nations might listen. It was up to him to find them.

Lavionkié started to stir. She rolled over and wrapped her arms around her lover's neck. She kissed him. Then she greeted him with an impassioned look.

"Good morning, my lovely Lavionkié," Radisson replied as he caressed her beaming face, her dark silky hair, her mink-like back, her exciting curves.

Life seemed simple when their gazes met, reflecting back the same shared happiness like two mirrors. But the reality they lived in was anything but simple.

"I have to go back to the fort today," Radisson added.

He still had to invite a few people to the Easter feast before he left. Lavionkié made a face as she snuggled into Radisson's arms. Radisson held her tightly.

"When will you be back?"

"In a day or two... There's going to be a big feast at the fort. You could come this time."

Lavionkié did not answer. She knew that her mother, who had little time for the French, would be against it. And yet Radisson was so kind, so warm, so strong. She could have spent the whole day in his arms. But she had to let go of him so that he could leave.

Radisson found Robert Racine and two other Frenchmen waiting impatiently for him outside the chapel. With the invitations made, they were now eager to get back to the safety of the fort. The journey took no time at all. The sentries opened the gate for them. All that remained was to proceed with the final preparations.

Commander Dupuys regularly sent out men to watch the river and the great lake of the Iroquois to keep an eye on the ice that covered them. Never had the French waited for spring to come with so much hope. They rejoiced as the blazing sun melted the snow. But they fretted every time the cool nights left a thin layer of ice on the water's surface. As soon as conditions seemed good enough to allow navigation, the signal was given.

Radisson could see that the two flat-bottomed boats were ready and covered in canvas beneath the birch-bark canoes, which had all been repaired. The bags had been sorted and packed up. Everything was ready for them to leave. Most of the French didn't mind having to leave valuables and pelts behind them, provided they escaped with their lives. Bringing everything with them was impossible. But Radisson looked bitterly at the fifty bundles of pelts that had been set to one side. So much effort for no reward. Another missed target.

Radisson met Father Ragueneau in the Jesuits' apartment.

"At last, there you are!" cried the Jesuit.

"Are you well, Father?"

"Very well, thank you. But it was high time for me to spring back into action."

The Jesuit had begun preparing the Easter celebrations.

"It hurt so much to be paralyzed for a whole month."

"Did Takanissorens visit you, as he promised?"

"Just once. He brought me tobacco and advised me to offer it up to the spirits. He says they were probably angry when I injured myself. That's how he sees my accident. I told him that our God liked tobacco, too, and that I'd be sure to make the offering. He seemed happy."

"Did you really hurt yourself, Father?"

"Not at all! I followed your plan to the letter. And may God help us see it through right to the end!"

"You seemed to be in so much pain that I feared you had really hurt yourself."

"I hurt my hip as I bumped up against a few rocks. That helped me cry out all the louder. But two days later, I didn't feel anything at all. Only this darned plaster, which has left me limping around. What an ordeal! It drove me mad to be here half paralyzed, even if there was nothing wrong with me. I took the opportunity to pray for us, morning, noon, and night."

"The surgeon played his role well. He didn't breathe a word to anyone?"

"As silent as the grave. And you're right: he played his role to perfection! I even wondered if I had really hurt myself when I saw him so upset. Any word of the hunters?"

"They will be back soon. We must leave."

"The men who keep an eye on the ice say we can travel along the river safely now. I suggest we celebrate Easter a week early, on Palm Sunday. The Iroquois won't suspect a thing, of course, and God won't hold it against us. If you don't have any objection, I ask that you set out immediately to warn all our missionaries and invite as many people as possible to the feast. Your idea of thanking the Iroquois spirits for my recovery at the same time should help attract a crowd. First and foremost, make sure no Frenchman will be held captive in the villages. Everything is ready here."

"I'll convince them, Father. I'll see to everything. Don't worry. The Iroquois won't want to miss an even bigger feast than Candlemas. They won't suspect a thing. Every single Frenchmen will be able to get away as planned."

"I hope so, Radisson. Did you let the people of Onondaga know?"

"I did. I told them their spirits must be favourable to us since you healed so quickly and that it would be the greatest feast of their lives. Many told me they would be there. Andoura will encourage them to come. It's going to work, Father. I'm sure of it."

"Go now. And take only men we can trust with you."

"Everything will be done as you intend, Father. I'll see you soon."

As Radisson left the room, Ragueneau called him back.

"Radisson!"

"Yes, Father?"

The Jesuit hesitated, but he considered it his duty to swallow his pride.

"Thank you for everything. You know that I do not approve of all your relationships with the Iroquois, but I must admit they have been indispensable. I knew that I would need you, but not to this extent. You managed to find a solution that, against all odds, is going to save us. Without a drop of blood being spilled. And you have put the plan into action like an expert. I congratulate you and I thank you on behalf of us all. I'm proud of you."

Surprised, Radisson accepted the praise humbly.

"I did it in part for you, Father. Even though you perhaps committed an error by coming here, you don't deserve that a single person should die because of your decision. It was a sound, bold project that could have brought us much. I have always supported you."

The fifty-two Frenchmen in Iroquois country were together at last. Father Le Mercier, who had travelled a great distance to get there, arrived last with a delegation of five Cayuga from his village. To play things safe, they didn't allow a single man or woman from the hundred or so Iroquois who had come to enter the fort, claiming that it was inappropriate to celebrate the feast of Easter inside fortified surroundings. The shelter outside the fort that had been used for Candlemas had been made bigger and more comfortable.

The celebrations began with a solemn mass sung by six Jesuit missionaries. During the sermon, Father Ragueneau thanked the Iroquois for having come celebrate with them the resurrection of the son of God, who reigned in heaven for all eternity, and sang the praises of the Iroquois spirits who had helped him get back on his feet. While convalescing, he said, he had a dream in which these spirits and the God of the French had become reconciled, granting extraordinary powers to all. He noted that the feast sought to make this dream a reality and to grant great powers to all. He encouraged them to honour their customs by eating everything the French put in front of them. If they did not, they would lose the opportunity to improve their people's lot.

Radisson was encouraged to see the Iroquois turn out in such numbers. On his way past, he had recognized many chiefs who were not favourable to the French, a sign that they had come to enjoy the feast and did not suspect a thing. Ragueneau's sermon was designed to encourage them to eat as much as they pleased, and then some more, in case the dream were to become reality and leave them with new powers. It was a case of mixing business with pleasure. Radisson also took it to be a good omen that they were celebrating the day when Christ miraculously escaped death.

When the sermon was over, Radisson returned to the fort to ensure the feast got underway right after the mass. The Iroquois could not be given a minute to think. Their greed had to get the better of them as quickly as possible. The orders he had given to everyone for the feast were clear: they had to be urged to eat and eat until they were left exhausted. The fate of the French depended on the Iroquois being gluttons.

As soon as he heard the final Latin blessing, Radisson led out a small procession carrying six pots of sagamité. They set them down in the shelter, to the Iroquois' great delight. Radisson rushed over to serve the chiefs he knew personally: Andoura, Awenissera, and Takanissorens, as well as his informer Ouatsouan, who naturally wasn't going to pass up an opportunity to get something for nothing from the French. Suddenly he saw Ononta. His stomach tied itself in knots as he realized his mistake. How had he missed him earlier? The shaman was staring suspiciously at the walls of the shelter, as though sensing something was being kept from him. Radisson swooped on him like an eagle.

"Hello, Ononta! How nice it is to see you again!"

The Iroquois hadn't seen him coming. Radisson didn't give him a chance to speak.

"Stay where you are! I'll bring you a bowl of sagamité right away! Don't let it be said I ever let my master serve himself on a day like today. Be thankful to the French, Ononta. You'll remember this feast until your dying day. I'm on my way! Just give me a minute!"

Radisson plunged a bowl down into the sagamité, grabbed a spoon on his way past, and rushed to hand it, still oozing, to Ononta.

"I'm sorry I didn't say hello earlier. Did you know Lavionkié and I are going to marry according to your customs? She makes me so happy! Eat to our happiness and enjoy the generosity of the French. I'll bring you anything you want."

"I heard about the Candlemas feast and didn't want to miss this one."

Radisson was already back in the fort giving more orders.

"Always serve the chiefs first and give them the finest cuts! I'll point them out to you. They're all there. Don't forget Ononta, the shaman! And don't scrimp on the portions! As long as their mouths are full, they won't be asking any questions."

At day's end, Radisson invited the Iroquois to take a break from eating by taking on the French in games of skill. (The French were under orders to let the Iroquois win so that they could bask in their superiority.) The French and the Iroquois then danced together Iroquois style. Next, the hosts sang their traditional, rousing songs. Their guests loved it. During the activities, men covered the floor of the shelter with fresh balsam boughs and then draped beaver pelts over them. When night fell, the Iroquois made themselves comfortable. Torches and fires were lit for light and warmth.

Radisson repeated his most important order.

"Not one Iroquois is to be allowed to rest his weary eyes, not even for a minute, do you hear me? Give them more to eat. Talk to them. Make plenty of noise. Walk past them. Slap their backs. Give them encouragement."

The night was much colder than the French had foreseen. Even with the fires raging, a few Iroquois began to shiver and complain. They asked for more pelts. Radisson gave orders not to hand them out: the cold would keep them awake.

123

"We are adding wood to the fire," the French replied. "We have no covers left and your pelts are all wrapped up. We'll bring you more to eat instead. That will warm you up!"

The guests helped themselves to generous portions of delicious, steaming stews that contained all the duck and Canada goose they had. The Iroquois were not new to such feasts and nibbled to save room for later.

Toward the end of the night, as the French gave the Iroquois a little time to digest, the fort's finest storytellers shouted their tales while others clowned around. Some of them took the Iroquois to task, pointing at them and asking them questions in French. The Iroquois tried but failed to understand.

"Thank you for coming!" they explained in Iroquois.

Just a little more effort. The celebrations were not over yet. There was still a lot of food left. Keep going! The spirits will be grateful.

The French took turns. While half of them rested inside the fort, the other half kept the Iroquois awake. The sun rose at last, its light re-energizing everyone.

There were shouts of joy when the French brought out three spit-roasted deer. The Iroquois had made proving their stamina a point of honour and kept on eating even though they no longer had any appetite. They had been through this before! And they were not going to break their own tradition on account of the French.

Back inside, the French had begun to gather the bags beside the gate that opened up onto the river. The Jesuits and Commander Dupuys were responsible for ensuring that everything went like clockwork and was ready on time. The canoes were brought one by one, then loaded. It would soon be time to leave.

The Jesuits joined the celebrations. They interrupted the feast for a moment to pray and sing with the guests. They had the Iroquois stand, one by one, to bless them. The time had come to preach the word of God to them one last time in their booming voices, with the fervour of one last chance. They walked among them to shake their hands, thanking them for helping to bring about an agreement between the Iroquois spirits and the God of the French. Father Le Moyne lingered with Awenissera. The old chief was uncomfortable because he could not warn his friend of the plot that would soon be the downfall of the French. Takanissorens was keeping a close eye on him to ensure he did not say too much. Awenissera was crying. Father Le Moyne understood why, but could not reveal anything either. He did his best to comfort him.

"Do not be sad, Awenissera. I am happy that you are celebrating the resurrection of our God with us. It is a moment I will never forget. We have done great things together, and we will have many more opportunities to celebrate together, I am sure. Our Great Spirit is hope. He will reward you for your good deeds."

The old chief nodded sadly. The Jesuit was also sad to be leaving behind a dear friend. Le Moyne then went over to say goodbye to Andoura, who had always remained loyal to the French. The other missionaries had good words for others, too, even their enemies. They wanted to leave a good impression, hoping one day to have a second chance to convert the Iroquois.

Radisson then led another Iroquois-style dance. Three Frenchmen beat the drums with all their might, beating and beating and shouting at the top of their voices. They made a real din. Radisson went to make sure that Ononta still posed no threat. Overcome by the celebrations, the shaman's body had been left so tired and heavy that he seemed to be permanently dozing off.

"Be strong!" Radisson shouted into his ears to wake him. "The celebrations are almost over. Eat for me and Lavionkié! To our happiness!"

Radisson then went in search of Andoura.

"Thank you. Our feast has been a great success. It was worth making at least one last try. Thank you for helping me. The French will perhaps be saved thanks to you. Tell Lavionkié I wish she could have been here with us. Tell her I love her..."

Andoura slurred his reply. He would eat right to the end to save the French, he said.

In fact, the best dishes of all were still to come, to finish off their guests and give the French a clear path.

At the end of the second day, they brought out turtles boiled in their shells, smoked sturgeon, and bear fat thickened with cornmeal. The Iroquois were served one dish at a time, with the French always claiming it was the last. Their allies were making themselves ill to honour their custom. Others held both hands over their mouths to keep in the food they had made such an effort to swallow. Some were forced to give in, their eyes rolled upward, their stomachs ready to explode. They had never seen such a lavish feast. A handful of Frenchmen played the drum, blew into a bugle, and danced like madmen to keep the Iroquois awake.

"Do you see how the French love you and honour you?" Radisson cried. "Do not sleep! Be strong! There's only one more dish to come!"

But the Iroquois had had their fill. They begged Radisson and the Jesuits to put them out of their agony.

"Have mercy! Let us sleep! That's enough! Enough!"

And so it was. The French agreed to bring an end to the celebrations with one final precaution.

It was even colder than the night before. As well as stirring the fires in front of the shelter, Radisson handed out enough pelts to keep the Iroquois warm until the Last Judgment. He wanted them to sleep like bears in winter. As they unwrapped all the beaver pelts they were unable to bring back to the colony, he could barely contain his anger. Even the pelts that belonged to him would have to be left behind. He had traded away all his goods in vain. A dead loss. But many people had lost even more.

The trip had been a waste from start to finish. The blacksmiths' tools, bellows, and anvil would also be abandoned, along with piles of farming and carpentry tools and even the powder they couldn't carry with them. Not to mention all the buildings they had put up... What a waste. It all left a bitter taste in Radisson's mouth. The sole consolation was being able to escape with their lives. And even then, many obstacles would have to be overcome before they ever reached Montréal.

To give themselves every chance, Radisson told the Iroquois not to head back to their villages until the French had given them valuable gifts when they woke up. He asked them to be patient, since the French needed to rest, too. Once he had bade them goodnight, his role as operations chief was over.

The gate to the fort closed behind him. Once the main entrance had been locked tightly, all the men gathered in the fort's biggest room, where Commander Dupuys took charge.

"There's no time to lose!" he cried. "Be sure to bring the bags you are entitled to and carry them to the boat you were assigned. As soon as we are ready, I will give the signal to leave. We will file out in silence. We will put our boats in the water, starting with the flat-bottomed boats, which will lead. The canoes will follow behind. Once we are beyond the bend that takes us out of sight of the fort, we will light torches to guide the way. But not before. There is too much risk the Iroquois might see us. Be careful—and silent! Every one of you must follow this instruction to the letter. Our lives depend on it."

"Why not massacre them before we leave?" shouted out René Dufresne, standing so that everyone could see him. "They won't catch us if they're dead! Who's with me?"

"Let's get them while they sleep!" a strapping man replied. "Death to the traitors!"

"Follow me!" cried Dufresne, grabbing his musket.

The six Jesuits leapt to their feet to block the way.

"I'm in charge here, not you!" Zacharie Dupuys cried.

Father Ragueneau walked right up to Dufresne until their chests were touching. His arms were outstretched and his eyes were furious.

"We came to this country to convert the Iroquois to the faith of Jesus Christ, not to massacre them! The cross of Christ is our only sword. Damn you if you kill a single one of them!"

"One more word out of you and I'll leave you here bound hand and foot," added Dupuys.

Dufresne hesitated, took a step back, looked at the commander and the Jesuits, then began to shout again.

"Our lives before the Iroquois'! Your plan is too risky. All I'm trying to do is protect us. The men agree."

Dupuys unsheathed his sword and waved it at the rebel.

"Shut up or you'll be the one dying!"

"We need to hold the fort," suggested Simon, another strapping man who stood up at the back. "Thirty men could stay here while the others fetch reinforcements. When they come back, we'll attack! Death to the Iroquois!"

Radisson intervened.

"Simon is right! I want to stay with him! I'm not afraid of starving to death or being tortured. I want to sacrifice my life for the honour of the French! All those willing to die with us raise your hands!"

No one moved. Even Dufresne was lost for words.

"Anyone who stays here has no chance of survival," Radisson went on. "Reinforcements will never arrive in time. And if you massacre the Iroquois who are outside, all the others will hunt you down to the ends of the earth. They know you. They'll find you, wherever you are, and roast you slowly over a fire!"

"Enough!" said Dupuys, still brandishing his sword. "I've heard enough! Any man who does not follow orders immediately will be thrown to the Iroquois! Gather your belongings! We're leaving!"

The rebels gave in. Better to flee like hunted animals than perish as nameless heroes, far from their own. Running away was the only way to escape with everyone's life.

The night was cold and windy. It began to snow.

As he lifted the heavy flat-bottomed boat that would lead the expedition with Dupuys, Ragueneau, and eight other men, Radisson was sorry he had to leave without a word of explanation to Lavionkié and Andoura. His plan had been a total secret, and it had worked like a charm. They were leaving without a trace. But the hearts of those he had loved would be filled with bitterness. Life could sometimes be thankless.

When they reached the shoreline, a nasty shock was waiting for them. Not only was it snowing heavily, but a layer of ice had formed on the water. Too bad. They would have to force their way through. The flat-bottomed boats were sturdy enough to clear a path for the birch-bark canoes. With the clouds masking the moon and the stars, the night was inky black. They had trouble slipping the boats into the water without making a sound. More than a few men were thigh deep in water before they could clamber on board. But they managed it. Now they were all moving forward on the river.

Progress in the total darkness was desperately slow. They feared they might wake the Iroquois at any moment. Two men were posted at the front of the flat-bottomed boat that took the lead and they smashed the ice with heavy sticks while six paddlers worked tirelessly to force a path through. At last they were around the first bend in the river and could light their torches. Radisson piloted the expedition from the first flat-bottomed boat, given his experience at the helm of the *Zeelhaen*, on Touchet's barge, and in Iroquois canoes. Robert Racine led the other boat. The six Jesuits travelled separately so that at least one of them would be able to explain to the colony's authorities why the Gannentaha mission had ended on such a sour note.

They travelled all night, despite the ice and the half-light, giving their all to put as much distance as possible between them and the Iroquois who would soon be awake. Daylight freed them from fears of capsizing and drowning. It became easier to navigate. The sunshine comforted the men, especially those whose legs had been in the icy water and who had almost frozen during the night. Little by little, the ice disappeared in the sun.

They had agreed to keep going until they reached the great lake of the Iroquois. The mighty spring thaw pushed the boats along at a surprising speed. The crews of the two flat-bottomed boats worked miracles every time there was a bend in the river, to avoid the party being swept against the trees and rocks.

The first Iroquois awoke. Their sole concern was to put more wood on the dying fires and return to the warmth of their furs. They were slowly recovering from the feast. The day was well underway and all was silent in the fort. The Iroquois supposed the French must still be asleep. That was fine with them. They would wait as long as they had to for their gifts.

The French reached the mouth of the river in record time. The day was drawing to a close. The waves on the lake were so big that they had to stop. They were so afraid of being hunted down and caught that they would rather have pressed on. But it was too risky in such weather, in such darkness. They beached the boats on a small island, where they felt relatively safe. Dupuys set up a system of nightwatchmen while small fires were lit on the side of the lake where the Iroquois would not see them easily. They spread out on the ground the twenty or so beaver pelts they had brought with them to keep warm. They ate leftovers from the feast. The night was again very cold.

In the first light of day, Dupuys, the Jesuits, Radisson, Racine, and some of the more experienced men consulted each other. The wind had died down, but the waves were still threatening. Too bad. They had no choice but to set off again immediately, in spite of the poor conditions. Radisson had asked to install a small retractable mast on the flat-bottomed boats, as on a barge. The wind was blowing in the right direction and the sail would pull them along as well as the paddles. The canoes were lighter and faster but had more trouble with the waves. As a precaution, they stayed close to the shoreline and kept together as a group.

They hoped they would not have to stop again before they reached the smattering of islands where the river flowed out of the great lake and into the St. Lawrence River. The moonlight helped them navigate at night, but the torches were kept permanently lit on the flat-bottomed boats to help them keep their bearings.

On the morning of the second day following the feast, the Iroquois chiefs held a council. They agreed to wait until the

French were well rested before receiving their gifts and returning home. But the long silence seemed strange. They decided to show their impatience by calling the French.

Awenissera cupped his hands around his mouth before the main gate and cried:

"Hu-llo! We are well rested now! We are waiting. Are you asleep?"

No answer. Only a small bell could be heard on the other side of the gate. Awenissera called out again.

"Can you hear me? Is anyone there?"

Still no answer. It looked as though the French had disappeared.

Takanissorens wanted to be sure. He suggested going inside to look around the fort. He put together a makeshift ladder, scaled to the top of the palisade, swung one leg over the spiked posts, and got a foothold on the parapet. He took a good, long look around, but there was no one to be seen. Not a sound to be heard, not a mark on the melting snow. Fear gripped him in the face of the inexplicable. He motioned to those waiting below to walk over to the main gate and he would let them in. Ever so carefully, he climbed back down from the parapet and walked over to the gate, which he hurriedly opened. A pig was tied up right beside it, a string of little bells around its neck.

Dozens of Iroquois poured into the fort, every one of them on high alert. They split into groups of ten or fifteen to inspect their surroundings. There was no sign of the French, not the slightest trace of them having been there. The canoes had disappeared into thin air. Takanissorens consulted Ononta the shaman about this marvel. How could the French have vanished? Where could they be?

"The Great Spirit of the French is more powerful than it seems I believed," concluded Ononta. "They have gone. They have escaped."

The French at last reached the river that led out of the great lake of the Iroquois. The tension came down a notch. Some set up a temporary camp, while others explored the maze of beautiful islands to find the best way to the St. Lawrence. The current was so powerful that it would be hard to come back in the flat-bottomed boats if they lost their way. A few Frenchmen stood watch in the evergreens that hid their camp. The others prepared something to eat and made provisions for the next part of the trip. It took them two days to find their way. They left at dawn with shouts of joy. This time, there was no way the Iroquois could catch them. They had shaken them off. They had gotten the better of them. The river in full spate was all that stood between them and Montréal.

"And that wasn't counting the ice and the awful rapids we had to cross," said Radisson. "The closer we got to Montréal, the less progress spring had made. We even had to break the ice with an axe at one point, the river was so frozen. Then the sun came out, it warmed up, and the ice suddenly fell away in great chunks. It was breaking up all around us, with a terrible cracking sound. Huge chunks of it floated past us in the current, banging against our boats, crashing into us. Any one of them might have crushed us, but God was with us. We made it home.

"We couldn't ever stop because the shore was still covered in ice. We had to push on. Ever onward. The water was so high that we floated over the rapids. The canoes had a rough time of it. One day, my boat got beached on a sandbank and filled with water. We managed to empty it and press on. A canoe capsized the very next day. Three men tried to swim to shore, but the waves and current were too strong... they drowned. God rest their souls. We saved the other two men, who had managed to cling to the canoe.

"They were the only men we lost. When we reached the Lachine rapids, we decided to stay in our boats and run the rapids. The day before, the rapids were still covered in ice, the people in Montréal told us. A day earlier and we'd all still be there, drowned beneath the ice. It was written in the stars that we would get away."

They had all gathered in Marguerite's house to listen to the story: Françoise and her husband, Claude Volant, Pierre Godefroy and his wife, the neighbour Lajeunesse, Marguerite and her new husband, Médard Chouart. Radisson had rested for a few days in Montréal, before going on to Trois-Rivières. He had arrived the day before. He was savouring his victory over the cunning Iroquois and the adversity they had faced. He couldn't have been happier as he recounted his adventure in the comfort and safety of the house he knew well, before an audience that was fascinated by the dangers he had overcome through his courage and skill.

Médard Chouart listened most attentively of all. He was also the man Radisson spoke to most enthusiastically. He was now known as Médard Chouart dit Des Groseilliers since returning from his perilous two-year journey to the Great Lakes. The governor himself had honoured him for saving the colony; heading three hundred Indians working with the French, both old and new allies, he had brought back more pelts than any man had ever set eyes on. He was rich now, and respected, and married to Marguerite, who had waited so long for him.

"Just as well we didn't massacre the Iroquois who took part in the Easter celebrations or else an army would be hot on our heels by now. We killed no one and will have time to organize our defences. Peace might even still stand a chance. Either way, our top priority was getting everyone back to the colony alive. And that's what we managed to do," Radisson concluded, eager to impress his new brother-in-law.

Pregnant with her third child, Marguerite was worried by the bad news Radisson brought with him. What Médard had seen in the Great Lakes painted the same picture. Tensions were threatening to boil over everywhere. War was likely going to start up again, with all the suffering that entailed. She went back to stirring the soup simmering over the fire, preferring not to think about Trois-Rivières once again being under siege, about the loss of her first husband to the fighting, and how so many others might once again have to pay the price.

Françoise couldn't help shedding a tear or two as she listened to her brother recount the dangers he had once again escaped. Claude Volant and Dandonneau dit Lajeunesse looked disheartened. They were thinking of the clashes that lay ahead. Pierre Godefroy could also see dark days to come. What he had warned of had happened more quickly than he would have thought possible. It didn't bode well for the French. Only Médard Chouart had a strange smile on his face. He had very much enjoyed the story told by his new brother-in-law. He liked hearing of Radisson's skill, his sang-froid, his cunning. Not just anyone could get the better of the Iroquois like he had. He was already fond of the young man.

On the other hand, he didn't understand how Radisson could still hope for peace. That seemed crazy to him. The very thought had made him laugh nervously. How would peace be possible in the topsy-turvy world he knew? Among the Hurons where he had served the Jesuits? In Trois-Rivières where he had fought the Iroquois? Or in the Great Lakes where dozens of nations watched each other like cats and dogs, ready to pounce and destroy each other?

He suddenly burst out laughing. All eyes turned to him in surprise. Radisson had the unpleasant feeling he was being laughed at. After the success he had known and the dangers he had overcome, he wasn't going to put up with being ridiculed, especially not from within his own family, not by a man he thought he had impressed.

"What's so funny?" he said, a threat more than a question.

But Des Groseilliers laughed all the more. The table was shaking.

"Stop it!"

Marguerite didn't have time to step in to reassure her brother. Radisson had already unsheathed his knife and was brandishing it at a giant of a man who knew no fear.

"I said STOP!" he cried, leaping to his feet.

But Des Groseilliers had seized Radisson by the wrist and was squeezing it so hard that Radisson could no longer move a muscle, let alone hold his knife. It clattered back down onto the table. Radisson fought hard not to cry out in pain. No one moved. Des Groseilliers had stopped laughing.

"I like you, dear brother-in-law," Médard told him.

Radisson hadn't seen it coming. Des Groseilliers stood up too, towering over the young man by a good head.

"I'm not laughing at you," explained the great brute. "I just think it's funny that you still believe in peace. If you'd seen what I've seen in the Great Lakes, you'd be less sure of yourself."

The two men sat back down. Pierre Godefroy, who had readily given up his position as captain of the militia to Des Groseilliers, knew just how much he'd proved his worth in many a clash. The Indians saw him as a great war chief, and the people of Trois-Rivières admired him for the feats of arms they had heard about him.

"It's the Iroquois offensive that made all our former allies flee to the Great Lakes," said Des Groseilliers. "And it was war again that made all these Indians return to the colony with me. They came looking for weapons to take their revenge. They want to fight the Iroquois, beat them, and return to the land of their ancestors. Everywhere I travelled, just one spark would be enough to set everything off. The Indians love war. The French, too'... So that's what I think of your peace. It's laughable!"

"It takes courage to fight for peace," Radisson replied with conviction. "And I have that courage! We have to believe. Peace is worth more to anyone than war will ever be."

Des Groseilliers sized up the young, resourceful man who had just appeared in his life.

"You're not wrong, Radisson. For trade, peace is better than war. And trade is my life. Does the fur trade mean anything to you?"

"Of course. It's the reason I came to New France! Trade is my life, too."

"What were you doing with the Jesuits then?"

"That was just circumstances. A setback along the way. But that's behind me now. I don't owe the Jesuits a thing."

Des Groseilliers ran a hand as broad as a paddle through his thick beard and looked Radisson square in the eyes, his gaze as piercing as any arrow.

"If I gave you the chance to go back to the Great Lakes with me to trade, what would you say?"

"I'd say I'm ready to leave tomorrow morning!"

Des Groseilliers nodded slowly.

"You and me are going to get along like a house on fire, Radisson. We're going to get along just fine."

HISTORIAN TURNED NOVELIST

THE FIRST TIME I read the six accounts of Radisson's travels, written by Radisson himself, I was studying history at university... and I couldn't get enough of them. I spent five years of my life studying the background of this exceptional man: his writing, the places he lived, the people he met. The findings of my research for my master's and PhD have been presented many times at science conferences and published in various forms. The resulting PhD thesis was published as *Pierre-Esprit Radisson, aventurier et commerçant, 1636-1710*, by Les éditions du Septentrion in 2001, and translated by Mary E. Brennan-Ricard as *Pierre-Esprit Radisson: Merchant, Adventurer, 1636-1710*, for McGill-Queen's University Press, in 2002. In other words, I am a historian, a specialist recognized by my peers on the life of Radisson.

When I began to write this series of adventure novels some years later (the first volume was published by Septentrion in 2011, then translated by Peter McCambridge for Baraka Books in 2012), I was careful to respect what I knew of Radisson as a professional historian. Even though my main aim is to write

exciting novels, I sprinkle them liberally with accurate histor-
ical information, working these details into the social and
cultural backdrop to Radisson's life. The series therefore aims
to entertain younger readers, all while broadening their knowledge and understanding of seventeenth-century history.

The man of flesh and blood who features in these novels,
brought to life by dreams, emotions, and very precise tastes,
naturally goes beyond what history can tell us about the real
Radisson who lived from 1636 to 1710. Here, the novelist takes
over from the historian and has to come up with what Radisson
might have thought, said, and felt on a daily basis. The novelist must also create secondary characters—some of whom
appear in Radisson's own writing—and have them interact
with each other. To do this, I base my stories on what history
knows of the people Radisson rubbed shoulders with—like the
Jesuit missionaries—as well as prevailing seventeenth-century
thinking, values, and behaviour in France, New France, and
among the First Nations.

In Volume 1 of *The Adventures of Radisson*, I faithfully followed the first account Radisson left us. It describes in detail
his experience living among the Mohawk nation of the Iroquois
people. I added a few episodes of my own, particularly during
the war expedition, which Radisson recounts rather briefly,
and I completed a number of other scenes using research
undertaken during my studies.

Volumes 2 and 3 were more problematic since Radisson had
written nothing of his time in France or his life in New France.
I chose to introduce readers to this ill-known part of his life
by imagining it for myself in order to better understand how
this extraordinary character developed and the reasons that
might have driven him to work for the austere Jesuits after
having led a much freer and very different life among the
Iroquois.

Volume 2, then, is a realistic (and thoroughly researched) depiction of how Radisson might have developed as an individual, as well as a precise overview of France and New France in the 1650s. These additions allowed me to examine the issues of the day in a period that determined the future of dozens of First Nations, and the future of New France. The Iroquois changing from war to peace and from peace to war again, for example, actually happened and is backed by solid documentary evidence.

Volume 3 is based on Radisson's second account of his travels. From here on in, the novel is again based on his writing, although the second travel diary is less complete than the first. This explains why, as an author, I had to take a few more liberties in Volumes 2 and 3 than I had in Volume 1. I emphasized Radisson's real-life inclination to work toward peace, for example, and I gave him the starring role in coming up with the strategy that led to the French fleeing Iroquois country. While he no doubt contributed to this strategy (documents from the time confirm this), he wasn't necessarily the driving force behind it.

In Volume 4, I'll be sticking closely to Radisson's very detailed account of his extraordinary journey to Lake Superior with Des Groseilliers. Radisson's peaceful tendencies will be tested to the limit when confrontation puts his life in danger.

Fiction and History from Baraka Books

YA FICTION

*The Adventures of Radisson
Vol. 1 Hell Never Burns
Vol. 2 – Back to the New World*
Martin Fournier

*Break Away 1 – Jessie on My Mind
Break Away 2 – Power Forward*
Sylvain Hotte

ADULT FICTION

The Raids, The Nickel Range Trilogy, Vol. 1
Mick Lowe

The Insatiable Maw, The Nickel Range Trilogy, Vol. 2
Mick Lowe

Speak to Me in Indian
David Gidmark

Washika
Robert A. Poirier

HISTORY

A People's History of Quebec
Jacques Lacoursière & Robin Philpot

*The History of Montréal
The Story of a Great North American City*
Paul-André Linteau

*Soldiers for Sale, German "Mercerneries" with the British
in Canada During the American Revolution*
Jean-Pierre Wilhelmy

*Journey to the Heart of the First Peoples Collections
Musées de la civilisation*
Marie-Paule Robitaille